THE BOOK C. THREE

The Book of Three *lay closed on the table. Taran had never been allowed to read the volume for himself; now he was sure it held more than Dallben chose to tell him. In the sun-filled room, with Dallben still meditating and showing no sign of stopping, Taran rose and moved through the shimmering beams. From the forest came the monotonous tick of a beetle.*

His hands reached for the cover. Taran gasped in pain and snatched them away. They smarted as if each of his fingers had been stung by hornets.

USBORNE MODERN CLASSICS

Introducing timeless stories to today's readers

THE **BOOK OF THREE**

High praise for *The Chronicles of Prydain*:

"The strongest high fantasy written for children in our times." *School Library Journal*

"A very fine fantasy-adventure with its roots in the Mabinogion...a quite compelling magic of its own." *Times Literary Supplement*

"An enchanting fantasy set in the imaginary country of Prydain and peopled with an intriguing cast of characters. Filled with exciting and valorous action, humour, and truth, the fantasy is completely convincing and has some of the appeal of the Narnia books." *ALA Booklist*

"Lloyd Alexander's triumph is that while his plots follow a slashing heroic pattern, his quest is into the subtleties of manhood itself. It is rare that high excitement yields such quiet wisdom." *New York Times*

"The fantasy has the depth and richness of a medieval tapestry, infinitely detailed and imaginative." *Saturday Review*

"An exalting experience for the fortunate children whose imaginations are ready for great fantasy." *The Horn Book*

LLOYD ALEXANDER

THE BOOK OF THREE

USBORNE MODERN CLASSICS

THE LAND

CAER DATHYL
GWYDION

MOUNT
DRAGON

BATTLE SCENE

RIVER YSTRAD FFLEWDDUR

ANNUVIN
ARAWN

SPIRAL CASTLE
ACHREN AND EILONWY

THE BOOK

For the children who listened, the grown-ups
who were patient, and especially Ann Durell

First published in this edition in 2018 by Usborne Publishing Ltd.,
Usborne House, 83-85 Saffron Hill, London EC1N 8RT, England.
www.usborne.com

Text copyright © 1964 by Lloyd Alexander.
Cover illustration by Joe McLaren. © Usborne Publishing, Ltd.
Inside illustrations copyright © 2004 by Alison Read.
Pronunciation Guide copyright © 1999 by Henry Holt and Company.
Reprinted by permission of Henry Holt and Company, LLC.
The right of Lloyd Alexander to be identified as author of this work
has been asserted by him in accordance with the Copyright, Designs
and Patents Act 1988.

The name Usborne and the devices ♕ ⊕ are Trade Marks of
Usborne Publishing Ltd.

This is a work of fiction. The characters, incidents, and dialogues are
products of the author's imagination and are not to be construed as real.
Any resemblance to actual events or persons, living or dead,
is entirely coincidental.

A CIP catalogue record for this book is available from the British Library.

ISBN 9781474943444

JFMAM JASOND/18   00312/7

Printed in the UK.

CHAPTER ONE

The Assistant Pig-Keeper

Taran wanted to make a sword; but Coll, charged with the practical side of his education, decided on horseshoes. And so it had been horseshoes all morning long. Taran's arms ached, soot blackened his face. At last he dropped the hammer and turned to Coll, who was watching him critically.

"Why?" Taran cried. "Why must it be for horseshoes? As if we had any horses!"

Coll was stout and round and his great bald head

glowed bright pink. "Lucky for the horses," was all he said, glancing at Taran's handiwork.

"I could do better at making a sword," Taran protested. "I know I could." And before Coll could answer, he snatched the tongs, flung a strip of red-hot iron to the anvil, and began hammering away as fast as he could.

"Wait, wait!" cried Coll. "That is not the way to go after it!"

Heedless of Coll, unable even to hear him above the din, Taran pounded harder than ever. Sparks sprayed the air. But the more he pounded, the more the metal twisted and buckled, until, finally, the iron sprang from the tongs and fell to the ground. Taran stared in dismay. With the tongs, he picked up the bent iron and examined it.

"Not quite the blade for a hero," Coll remarked.

"It's ruined," Taran glumly agreed. "It looks like a sick snake," he added ruefully.

"As I tried telling you," said Coll, "you had it all wrong. You must hold the tongs—so. When you strike, the strength must flow from your shoulder and your wrist be loose. You can hear it when you do it right. There is a kind of music in it. Besides," he added, "this is not the metal for weapons."

Coll returned the crooked, half-formed blade to the furnace, where it lost its shape entirely.

"I wish I might have my own sword," Taran sighed, "and

you would teach me sword fighting."

"Wisht!" cried Coll. "Why should you want to know that? We have no battles at Caer Dallben."

"We have no horses, either," objected Taran, "but we're making horseshoes."

"Get on with you," said Coll, unmoved. "That is for practice."

"And so would this be," Taran urged. "Come, teach me the sword fighting. You must know the art."

Coll's shining head glowed even brighter. A trace of a smile appeared on his face, as though he were savouring something pleasant. "True," he said quietly, "I have held a sword once or twice in my day."

"Teach me now," pleaded Taran. He seized a poker and brandished it, slashing at the air and dancing back and forth over the hard packed earthen floor. "See," he called, "I know most of it already."

"Hold your hand," chuckled Coll. "If you were to come against me like that, with all your posing and bouncing, I should have you chopped into bits by this time." He hesitated a moment. "Look you," he said quickly, "at least you should know there is a right way and a wrong way to go about it."

He picked up another poker. "Here now," he ordered, with a sooty wink, "stand like a man."

Taran brought up his poker. While Coll shouted

instructions, they set to parrying and thrusting, with much banging, clanking, and commotion. For a moment Taran was sure he had the better of Coll, but the old man spun away with amazing lightness of foot. Now it was Taran who strove desperately to ward off Coll's blows.

Abruptly, Coll stopped. So did Taran, his poker poised in mid-air. In the doorway of the forge stood the tall, bent figure of Dallben.

Dallben, master of Caer Dallben, was three hundred and seventy-nine years old. His beard covered so much of his face he seemed always to be peering over a grey cloud. On the little farm, while Taran and Coll saw to the ploughing, sowing, weeding, reaping, and all the other tasks of husbandry, Dallben undertook the meditating, an occupation so exhausting he could accomplish it only by lying down and closing his eyes. He meditated an hour and a half following breakfast and again later in the day. The clatter from the forge had roused him from his morning meditation; his robe hung askew over his bony knees.

"Stop that nonsense directly," said Dallben. "I am surprised at you," he added, frowning at Coll. "There is serious work to be done."

"It wasn't Coll," Taran interrupted. "It was I who asked to learn swordplay."

"I did not say I was surprised at *you*," remarked Dallben.

"But perhaps I am, after all. I think you had best come with me."

Taran followed the ancient man out of the forge, across the chicken run, and into the white, thatched cottage. There, in Dallben's chamber, mouldering tomes overflowed the sagging shelves and spilled onto the floor amid heaps of iron cook-pots, studded belts, harps with or without strings, and other oddments.

Taran took his place on the wooden bench, as he always did when Dallben was in a mood for giving lessons or reprimands.

"I fully understand," said Dallben, settling himself behind his table, "in the use of weapons, as in everything else, there is a certain skill. But wiser heads than yours will determine when you should learn it."

"I'm sorry," Taran began, "I should not have..."

"I am not angry," Dallben said, raising a hand. "Only a little sad. Time flies quickly; things always happen sooner than one expects. And yet," he murmured, almost to himself, "it troubles me. I fear the Horned King may have some part in this."

"The Horned King?" asked Taran.

"We shall speak of him later," said Dallben. He drew a ponderous, leather-bound volume towards him, *The Book of Three*, from which he occasionally read to Taran and which, the boy believed, held in its pages everything anyone could possibly want to know.

"As I have explained to you before," Dallben went on, "– and you have very likely forgotten – Prydain is a land of many cantrevs – of small kingdoms – and many kings. And, of course, their war-leaders who command the warriors."

"But there is the High King above them all," said Taran, "Math Son of Mathonwy. His war-leader is the mightiest hero in Prydain. You told me of him. Prince Gwydion! Yes," Taran went on eagerly, "I know..."

"There are other things you do *not* know," Dallben said, "for the obvious reason that I have not told you. For the moment I am less concerned with the realms of the living than with the Land of the Dead, with Annuvin."

Taran shuddered at the word. Even Dallben had spoken it in a whisper.

"And with King Arawn, Lord of Annuvin," Dallben said. "Know this," he continued quickly, "Annuvin is more than a land of death. It is a treasure-house, not only of gold and jewels but of all things of advantage to men. Long ago, the race of men owned these treasures. By craft and deceit, Arawn stole them, one by one, for his own evil uses. Some few of the treasures have been wrested from him though most lie hidden deep in Annuvin, where Arawn guards them jealously."

"But Arawn did not become ruler of Prydain," Taran said.

"You may be thankful he did not," said Dallben. "He

would have ruled had it not been for the Children of Don, the sons of the Lady Don and her consort Belin, King of the Sun. Long ago they voyaged to Prydain from the Summer Country and found the land rich and fair, though the race of men had little for themselves. The Sons of Don built their stronghold at Caer Dathyl, far north in the Eagle Mountains. From there, they helped regain at least a portion of what Arawn had stolen, and stood as guardians against the lurking threat of Annuvin."

"I hate to think what would have happened if the Sons of Don hadn't come," Taran said. "It was a good destiny that brought them."

"I am not always sure," said Dallben, with a wry smile. "The men of Prydain came to rely on the strength of the House of Don as a child clings to its mother. They do so even today. Math, the High King, is descended from the House of Don. So is Prince Gwydion. But that is all by the way. Prydain has been at peace — as much as men can be peaceful — until now.

"What you do not know," Dallben said, "is this: it has reached my ears that a new and mighty war lord has risen, as powerful as Gwydion; some say more powerful. But he is a man of evil for whom death is a black joy. He sports with death as you might sport with a dog."

"Who is he?" cried Taran.

Dallben shook his head. "No man knows his name, nor

has any man seen his face. He wears an antlered mask, and for this reason he is called the Horned King. His purposes I do not know. I suspect the hand of Arawn, but in what manner I cannot tell. I tell you now for your own protection," Dallben added. "From what I saw this morning, your head is full of nonsense about feats of arms. Whatever notions you may have, I advise you to forget them immediately. There is unknown danger abroad. You are barely on the threshold of manhood, and I have a certain responsibility to see that you reach it, preferably with a whole skin. So, you are not to leave Caer Dallben under any circumstances, not even past the orchard, and certainly not into the forest – not for the time being."

"For the time being!" Taran burst out. "I think it will always be for the time being, and it will be vegetables and horseshoes all my life!"

"Tut," said Dallben, "there are worse things. Do you set yourself to be a glorious hero? Do you believe it is all flashing swords and galloping about on horses? As for being glorious..."

"What of Prince Gwydion?" cried Taran. "Yes! I wish I might be like him!"

"I fear," Dallben said, "that is entirely out of the question."

"But why?" Taran sprang to his feet. "I know if I had the chance..."

"Why?" Dallben interrupted. "In some cases," he said, "we learn more by looking for the answer to a question and not finding it than we do from learning the answer itself. This is one of those cases. I could tell you why, but at the moment it would only be more confusing. If you grow up with any kind of sense – which you sometimes make me doubt – you will very likely reach your own conclusions.

"They will probably be wrong," he added. "However, since they will be yours, you will feel a little more satisfied with them."

Taran sank back and sat, gloomy and silent, on the bench. Dallben had already begun meditating again. His chin gradually came to rest on his collarbone; his beard floated around his ears like a fog bank; and he began snoring peacefully.

The spring scent of apple blossom drifted through the open window. Beyond Dallben's chamber, Taran glimpsed the pale green fringe of forest. The fields, ready to cultivate, would soon turn golden with summer. *The Book of Three* lay closed on the table. Taran had never been allowed to read the volume for himself; now he was sure it held more than Dallben chose to tell him. In the sun-filled room, with Dallben still meditating and showing no sign of stopping, Taran rose and moved through the shimmering beams. From the forest came the monotonous tick of a beetle.

His hands reached for the cover. Taran gasped in pain and snatched them away. They smarted as if each of his fingers had been stung by hornets. He jumped back, stumbled against the bench, and dropped to the floor, where he put his fingers woefully into his mouth.

Dallben's eyes blinked open. He peered at Taran and yawned slowly. "You had better see Coll about a lotion for those hands," he advised. "Otherwise, I shouldn't be surprised if they blistered."

Fingers smarting, the shamefaced Taran hurried from the cottage and found Coll near the vegetable garden.

"You have been at *The Book of Three*," Coll said. "That is not hard to guess. Now you know better. Well, that is one of the three foundations of learning: see much, study much, suffer much." He led Taran to the stable where medicines for the livestock were kept, and poured a concoction over Taran's fingers.

"What is the use of studying much when I'm to see nothing at all?" Taran retorted. "I think there is a destiny laid on me that I am not to know anything interesting, or do anything interesting. I'm certainly not to *be* anything. I'm not anything even at Caer Dallben!"

"Very well," said Coll, "if that is all that troubles you, I shall make you something. From this moment, you are Taran, Assistant Pig-Keeper. You shall help me take care of Hen Wen: see her trough is full, carry her water, and give her a good scrubbing every other day."

"That's what I do now," Taran said bitterly.

"All the better," said Coll, "for it makes things that much easier. If you want to be something with a name attached to it, I can't think of anything closer to hand. And it is not every lad who can be assistant keeper to an oracular pig. Indeed, she is the only oracular pig in Prydain, and the most valuable."

"Valuable to Dallben," Taran said. "She never tells *me* anything."

"Did you think she would?" replied Coll. "With Hen Wen, you must know how to ask — here, what was that?" Coll shaded his eyes with his hand. A black, buzzing cloud streaked from the orchard, and bore on so rapidly and passed so close to Coll's head that he had to leap out of the way.

"The bees!" Taran shouted. "They're swarming."

"It is not their time," cried Coll. "There is something amiss."

The cloud rose high towards the sun. An instant later Taran heard a loud clucking and squawking from the chicken run. He turned to see the five hens and the rooster beating their wings. Before it occurred to him they were attempting to fly, they, too, were aloft.

Taran and Coll raced to the chicken run, too late to catch the fowls. With the rooster leading, the chickens flapped awkwardly through the air and disappeared over the brow of a hill.

From the stable the pair of oxen bellowed and rolled their eyes in terror.

Dallben's head poked out of the window. He looked irritated. "It has become absolutely impossible for any kind of meditation whatsoever," he said, with a severe glance at Taran. "I have warned you once..."

"Something frightened the animals," Taran protested. "First the bees, then the chickens flew off..."

Dallben's face turned grave. "I have been given no knowledge of this," he said to Coll. "We must ask Hen Wen about it immediately, and we shall need the letter sticks. Quickly, help me find them."

Coll moved hastily to the cottage door. "Watch Hen Wen closely," he ordered Taran. "Do not let her out of your sight."

Coll disappeared inside the cottage to search for Hen Wen's letter sticks, the long rods of ash wood carved with spells. Taran was both frightened and excited. Dallben, he knew, would consult Hen Wen only on a matter of greatest urgency. Within Taran's memory, it had never happened before. He hurried to the pen.

Hen Wen usually slept until noon. Then, trotting daintily, despite her size, she would move to a shady corner of her enclosure and settle comfortably for the rest of the day. The white pig was continually grunting and chuckling to herself, and whenever she saw Taran, she would raise her wide, cheeky face so that he could scratch under her chin. But this time, she paid no attention to him. Wheezing and whistling, Hen Wen was digging furiously in the soft earth at the far side of the pen, burrowing so rapidly she would soon be out.

Taran shouted at her, but the clods continued flying at a great rate. He swung himself over the fence. The oracular pig stopped and glanced around. As Taran approached the hole, already sizeable, Hen Wen hurried to the opposite side of the pen and started a new excavation.

Taran was strong and long-legged, but, to his dismay, he saw that Hen Wen moved faster than he. As soon as he chased her from the second hole, she turned quickly on her short legs and made for the first. Both, by now, were big enough for her head and shoulders.

Taran frantically began scraping earth back into the burrow. Hen Wen dug faster than a badger, her hind legs planted firmly, her front legs ploughing ahead. Taran despaired of stopping her. He scrambled back over the rails and jumped to the spot where Hen Wen was about to emerge, planning to seize her and hang on until Dallben and Coll arrived. He underestimated Hen Wen's speed and strength.

In an explosion of dirt and pebbles, the pig burst from under the fence, heaving Taran into the air. He landed with the wind knocked out of him. Hen Wen raced across the field and into the woods.

Taran followed. Ahead, the forest rose up dark and threatening. He took a breath and plunged after her.

CHAPTER TWO

The Mask of the King

Hen Wen had vanished. Ahead, Taran heard a thrashing among the leaves. The pig, he was sure, was keeping out of sight in the bushes. Following the sound, he ran forwards. After a time the ground rose sharply, forcing him to clamber on hands and knees up a wooded slope. At the crest the forest broke off before a meadow. Taran caught a glimpse of Hen Wen dashing into the waving grass. Once across the meadow, she disappeared beyond a stand of trees.

Taran hurried after her. This was farther than he had

ever dared venture, but he struggled on through the heavy undergrowth. Soon, a fairly wide trail opened, allowing him to quicken his pace. Hen Wen had either stopped running or had outdistanced him. He heard nothing but his own footsteps.

He followed the trail for some while, intending to use it as a landmark on the way back, although it twisted and branched off so frequently he was not at all certain in which direction Caer Dallben lay.

In the meadow Taran had been flushed and perspiring. Now he shivered in the silence of oaks and elms. The woods here were not thick, but shadows drenched the high tree trunks and the sun broke through only in jagged streaks. A damp green scent filled the air. No bird called; no squirrel chattered. The forest seemed to be holding its breath.

Yet there was, beneath the silence, a groaning restlessness and a trembling among the leaves. The branches twisted and grated against each other like broken teeth. The path wavered under Taran's feet, and he felt desperately cold. He flung his arms around himself and moved more quickly to shake off the chill. He was, he realized, running aimlessly; he could not keep his mind on the forks and turns of the path.

He halted suddenly. Hoofbeats thudded in front of him. The forest shook as they grew louder. In another moment a black horse burst into view.

Taran fell back, terrified. Astride the foam-spattered

animal rode a monstrous figure. A crimson cloak flamed from his naked shoulders. Crimson stained his gigantic arms. Horror-stricken, Taran saw not the head of a man but the antlered head of a stag.

The Horned King! Taran flung himself against an oak to escape the flying hoofs and the heaving, glistening flanks. Horse and rider swept by. The mask was a human skull; from it, the great antlers rose in cruel curves. The Horned King's eyes blazed behind the gaping sockets of whitened bone.

Many horsemen galloped in his train. The Horned King uttered the long cry of a wild beast, and his riders took it up as they streamed after him. One of them, an ugly, grinning warrior, caught sight of Taran. He turned his mount and drew a sword. Taran sprang from the tree and plunged into the underbrush. The blade followed, hissing like an adder. Taran felt it sting across his back.

He ran blindly, while saplings whipped his face and hidden rocks jutted out to pitch him forwards and stab at his knees. Where the woods thinned, Taran clattered along a dry stream bed until, exhausted, he stumbled and held out his hands against the whirling ground.

The sun had already dipped westwards when Taran opened his eyes. He was lying on a stretch of turf with a cloak thrown over him. One shoulder smarted painfully. A man kneeled beside him. Nearby, a white horse cropped the grass. Still dazed, fearful the riders had overtaken him, Taran started up. The man held out a flask.

"Drink," he said. "Your strength will return in a moment."

The stranger had the shaggy, grey-streaked hair of a wolf. His eyes were deep-set, flecked with green. Sun and wind had leathered his broad face, burned it dark and grained it with fine lines. His cloak was coarse and travel-stained. A wide belt with an intricately wrought buckle circled his waist.

"Drink," the stranger said again, while Taran took the flask dubiously. "You look as though I were trying to poison you." He smiled. "It is not thus that Gwydion Son of Don deals with a wounded..."

"Gwydion!" Taran choked on the liquid and stumbled to his feet. "You are not Gwydion!" he cried. "I know of him. He is a great war-leader, a hero! He is not..." His eyes fell on the long sword at the stranger's belt. The golden pommel was smooth and rounded, its colour deliberately muted; ash leaves of pale gold entwined at the hilt, and a pattern of leaves covered the scabbard. It was truly the weapon of a prince.

Taran dropped to one knee and bowed his head. "Lord Gwydion," he said, "I did not intend insolence." As Gwydion helped him rise, Taran still stared in disbelief at the simple attire and the worn, lined face. From all Dallben had told

24

him of this glorious hero, from all he had pictured to himself – Taran bit his lips.

Gwydion caught Taran's look of disappointment. "It is not the trappings that make the prince," he said gently, "nor, indeed, the sword that makes the warrior. Come," he ordered, "tell me your name and what happened to you. And do not ask me to believe you got a sword wound picking gooseberries or poaching hares."

"I saw the Horned King!" Taran burst out. "His men ride the forest; one of them tried to kill me. I saw the Horned King himself! It was horrible, worse than Dallben told me!"

Gwydion's eyes narrowed. "Who are you?" he demanded. "Who are you to speak of Dallben?"

"I am Taran of Caer Dallben," Taran answered, trying to appear bold but succeeding only in turning paler than a mushroom.

"Of Caer Dallben?" Gwydion paused an instant and gave Taran a strange glance. "What are you doing so far from there? Does Dallben know you are in the forest? Is Coll with you?"

Taran's jaw dropped and he looked so thunderstruck that Gwydion threw back his head and burst into laughter.

"You need not be so surprised," Gwydion said. "I know Coll and Dallben well. And they are too wise to let you wander here alone. Have you run off, then? I warn you; Dallben is not one to be disobeyed."

"It was Hen Wen," Taran protested. "I should have known I couldn't hold on to her. Now she's gone, and it's my fault. I'm Assistant Pig-Keeper..."

"Gone?" Gwydion's face tightened. "Where? What has happened to her?"

"I don't know," Taran cried. "She's somewhere in the forest." As he poured out an account of the morning's events, Gwydion listened intently.

"I had not foreseen this," Gwydion murmured, when Taran had finished. "My mission fails if she is not found quickly." He turned abruptly to Taran. "Yes," he said, "I, too, seek Hen Wen."

"You?" cried Taran. "You came this far..."

"I need information she alone possesses," Gwydion said quickly. "I have journeyed a month from Caer Dathyl to get it. I have been followed, spied on, hunted. And now," he added with a bitter laugh, "she has run off. Very well. She will be found. I must discover all she knows of the Horned King." Gwydion hesitated. "I fear he himself searches for her even now.

"It must be so," he continued. "Hen Wen sensed him near Caer Dallben and fled in terror..."

"Then we should stop him," Taran declared. "Attack him, strike him down! Give me a sword and I will stand with you!"

"Gently, gently," chided Gwydion. "I do not say my life

26

is worth more than another man's, but I prize it highly. Do you think a lone warrior and one Assistant Pig-Keeper dare attack the Horned King and his war band?"

Taran drew himself up. "I would not fear him."

"No?" said Gwydion. "Then you are a fool. He is the man most to be dreaded in all Prydain. Will you hear something I learned during my journey, something even Dallben may not yet realize?"

Gwydion kneeled on the turf. "Do you know the craft of weaving? Thread by thread, the pattern forms." As he spoke, he plucked at the long blades of grass, knotting them to form a mesh.

"That is cleverly done," said Taran, watching Gwydion's rapidly moving fingers. "May I look at it?"

"There is a more serious weaving," said Gwydion, slipping the net into his own jacket. "You have seen one thread of a pattern loomed in Annuvin.

"Arawn does not long abandon Annuvin," Gwydion continued, "but his hand reaches everywhere. There are chieftains whose lust for power goads them like a sword point. To certain of them, Arawn promises wealth and dominion, playing on their greed as a bard plays on a harp. Arawn's corruption burns every human feeling from their hearts and they become his liege men, serving him beyond the borders of Annuvin and bound to him for ever."

"And the Horned King...?"

Gwydion nodded. "Yes. I know beyond question that he has sworn his allegiance to Arawn. He is Arawn's avowed champion. Once again, the power of Annuvin threatens Prydain."

Taran could only stare, speechless.

Gwydion turned to him. "When the time is ripe, the Horned King and I will meet. And one of us will die. That is my oath. But his purpose is dark and unknown, and I must learn it from Hen Wen."

"She can't be far," Taran cried. "I'll show you where she disappeared. I think I can find the place. It was just before the Horned King..."

Gwydion gave him a hard smile. "Do you have the eyes of an owl, to find a trail at nightfall? We sleep here and I shall be off at first light. With good luck, I may have her back before..."

"What of me?" Taran interrupted. "Hen Wen is in my charge. I let her escape and it is I who must find her."

"The task counts more than the one who does it," said Gwydion. "I will not be hindered by an Assistant Pig-Keeper, who seems eager to bring himself to grief." He stopped short and looked wryly at Taran. "On second thought, it appears I will. If the Horned King rides towards Caer Dallben, I cannot send you back alone and I dare not go with you and lose a day's tracking. You cannot stay in this forest by yourself. Unless I find some way..."

"I swear I will not hinder you," cried Taran. "Let me go with you. Dallben and Coll will see I can do what I set out to do!"

"Have I another choice?" asked Gwydion. "It would seem, Taran of Caer Dallben, we follow the same path. For a little while at least."

The white horse trotted up and nuzzled Gwydion's hand. "Melyngar reminds me it is time for food," Gwydion said. He unpacked provisions from the saddlebags. "Make no fire tonight," he warned. "The Horned King's outriders may be close at hand."

Taran swallowed a hurried meal. Excitement robbed him of appetite and he was impatient for dawn. His wound had stiffened so that he could not settle himself on the roots and pebbles. It had never occurred to him until now that a hero would sleep on the ground.

Gwydion, watchful, sat with his knees drawn up, his back against an enormous elm. In the lowering dusk Taran could barely distinguish the man from the tree; and could have walked within a pace of him before realizing he was any more than a splotch of shadow. Gwydion had sunk into the forest itself; only his green-flecked eyes shone in the reflection of the newly risen moon.

Gwydion was silent and thoughtful for a long while. "So you are Taran of Caer Dallben," he said at last. His voice from the shadows was quiet but urgent. "How long have you been with Dallben? Who are your kinsmen?"

Taran, hunched against a tree root, pulled his cloak closer about his shoulders. "I have always lived at Caer Dallben," he said. "I don't think I have any kinsmen. I don't know who my parents were. Dallben has never told me. I suppose," he added, turning his face away, "I don't even know who *I* am."

"In a way," answered Gwydion, "that is something we must all discover for ourselves. Our meeting was fortunate," he went on. "Thanks to you, I know a little more than I did, and you have spared me a wasted journey to Caer Dallben. It makes me wonder," Gwydion went on, with a laugh that was not unkind, "is there a destiny laid on me that an Assistant Pig-Keeper should help me in my quest?" He hesitated. "Or," he mused, "is it perhaps the other way around?"

"What do you mean?" Taran asked.

"I am not sure," said Gwydion. "It makes no difference. Sleep now, for we rise early tomorrow."

CHAPTER THREE

Gurgi

By the time Taran woke, Gwydion had already saddled Melyngar. The cloak Taran had slept in was damp with dew. Every joint ached from his night on the hard ground. With Gwydion's urging, Taran stumbled towards the horse, a white blur in the grey⁄pink dawn. Gwydion hauled Taran into the saddle behind him, spoke a quiet command, and the white steed moved quickly into the rising mist.

Gwydion was seeking the spot where Taran had last seen Hen Wen. But long before they had reached it, he reined up Melyngar and dismounted. As Taran watched, Gwydion kneeled and sighted along the turf.

"Luck is with us," he said. "I think we have struck her trail." Gwydion pointed to a faint circle of trampled grass. "Here she slept, and not too long ago." He strode a few paces forwards, scanning every broken twig and blade of grass.

Despite Taran's disappointment at finding the Lord Gwydion dressed in a coarse jacket and mud-spattered boots, he followed the man with growing admiration. Nothing, Taran saw, escaped Gwydion's eyes. Like a lean, grey wolf, he moved silently and easily. A little way on, Gwydion stopped, raised his shaggy head, and narrowed his eyes towards a distant ridge.

"The trail is not clear," he said, frowning. "I can only guess she might have gone down the slope."

"With all the forest to run in," Taran queried, "how can we begin to search? She might have gone anywhere in Prydain."

"Not quite," answered Gwydion. "I may not know where she went, but I can be sure where she did *not* go." He pulled a hunting knife from his belt. "Here, I will show you."

Gwydion kneeled and quickly traced lines in the earth. "These are the Eagle Mountains," he said, with a touch of longing in his voice, "in my own land of the north. Here, Great Avren flows. See how it turns west before it reaches the sea. We may have to cross it before our search ends. And this is the River Ystrad. Its valley leads north to Caer Dathyl.

"But see here," Gwydion went on, pointing to the left of the line he had drawn for the River Ystrad, "here is Mount Dragon and the domain of Arawn. Hen Wen would shun this above all. She was too long a captive in Annuvin; she would never venture near it."

"Was Hen in Annuvin?" Taran asked with surprise. "But how..."

"Long ago," Gwydion said, "Hen Wen lived among the race of men. She belonged to a farmer who had no idea at all of her powers. And so she might have spent her days as any ordinary pig. But Arawn knew her to be far from ordinary, and of such value that he himself rode out of Annuvin and seized her. What dire things happened while she was prisoner of Arawn – it is better not to speak of them."

"Poor Hen," Taran said, "it must have been terrible for her. But how did she escape?"

"She did not escape," said Gwydion. "She was rescued. A warrior went alone into the depths of Annuvin and brought her back safely."

"That was a brave deed!" Taran cried. "I wish that I..."

"The bards of the north still sing of it," Gwydion said. "His name shall never be forgotten."

"Who was it?" Taran demanded.

Gwydion looked closely at him. "Do you not know?" he asked. "Dallben has neglected your education. It was Coll," he said. "Coll Son of Collfrewr."

"Coll!" Taran cried. "Not the same..."

"The same," said Gwydion.

"But...but..." Taran stammered. "Coll? A hero? But...he's so bald!"

Gwydion laughed and shook his head. "Assistant Pig-Keeper," he said, "you have curious notions about heroes. I have never known courage to be judged by the length of a man's hair. Or, for the matter of that, whether he has any hair at all."

Crestfallen, Taran peered at Gwydion's map and said no more.

"Here," continued Gwydion, "not far from Annuvin, lies Spiral Castle. This, too, Hen Wen would avoid at all cost. It is the abode of Queen Achren. She is as dangerous as Arawn himself; as evil as she is beautiful. But there are secrets concerning Achren which are better left untold.

"I am sure," Gwydion went on, "Hen Wen will not go towards Annuvin or Spiral Castle. From what little I can see, she has run straight ahead. Quickly now, we shall try to pick up her trail."

Gwydion turned Melyngar towards the ridge. As they reached the bottom of the slope, Taran heard the waters of Great Avren rushing like wind in a summer storm.

"We must go again on foot," Gwydion said. "Her tracks may show somewhere along here, so we had best move slowly and carefully. Stay close behind me," he ordered. "If you start dashing ahead — and you seem to have that tendency — you will trample out any signs she might have left."

Taran obediently walked a few paces behind. Gwydion made no more sound than the shadow of a bird. Melyngar herself stepped quietly; hardly a twig snapped under her hoofs. Try as he would, Taran could not go as silently. The more careful he attempted to be, the louder the leaves rattled and crackled. Wherever he put his foot, there seemed to be a hole or spiteful branch to trip him up. Even Melyngar turned and gave him a reproachful look.

Taran grew so absorbed in not making noise that he soon lagged far behind Gwydion. On the slope, Taran believed he could make out something round and white. He yearned to be the first to find Hen Wen and he turned aside, clambered through the weeds — to discover nothing more than a boulder.

Disappointed, Taran hastened to catch up with Gwydion. Overhead, the branches rustled. As he stopped and looked up, something fell heavily to the ground behind him. Two hairy and powerful hands locked around his throat.

Whatever had seized him made barking and snorting noises. Taran forced out a cry for help. He struggled with his unseen opponent, twisting, flailing his legs, and throwing himself from one side to the other.

Suddenly he could breathe again. A shape sailed over his head and crashed against a tree trunk. Taran dropped to the ground and began rubbing his neck. Gwydion stood beside him. Sprawled under the tree was the strangest creature Taran had ever seen. He could not be sure whether it was animal or human. He decided it was both. Its hair was so matted and covered with leaves that it looked like an owl's nest in need of housecleaning. It had long, skinny, woolly arms, and a pair of feet as flexible and grimy as its hands.

Gwydion was watching the creature with a look of severity and annoyance. "So it is you," he said. "I ordered you not to hinder me or anyone under my protection."

At this, the creature set up a loud and piteous whining, rolled his eyes, and beat the ground with his palms.

"It is only Gurgi," Gwydion said. "He is always lurking about one place or another. He is not half as ferocious as he looks, nor a quarter as fierce as he should like to be, and more a nuisance than anything else. Somehow, he manages to see most of what happens, and he might be able to help us."

Taran had just begun to catch his breath. He was covered with Gurgi's shedding hair, in addition to the distressing odour of a wet wolfhound.

"O mighty prince," the creature wailed, "Gurgi is sorry;

and now he will be smacked on his poor, tender head by the strong hands of this great lord, with fearsome smackings. Yes, yes, that is always the way of it with poor Gurgi. But what honour to be smacked by the greatest of warriors!"

"I have no intention of smacking your poor, tender head," said Gwydion. "But I may change my mind if you do not leave off that whining and snivelling."

"Yes, powerful lord!" Gurgi cried. "See how he obeys rapidly and instantly!" He began crawling about on hands and knees with great agility. Had Gurgi owned a tail, Taran was sure he would have wagged it frantically.

"Then," Gurgi pleaded, "the two strengthful heroes will give Gurgi something to eat? Oh, joyous crunchings and munchings!"

"Afterwards," said Gwydion. "When you have answered our questions."

"Oh, afterwards!" cried Gurgi. "Poor Gurgi can wait, long, long for his crunchings and munchings. Many years from now, when the great princes revel in their halls — what feastings — they will remember hungry, wretched Gurgi waiting for them."

"How long you wait for your crunchings and munchings," Gwydion said, "depends on how quickly you tell us what we want to know. Have you seen a white pig this morning?"

A crafty look gleamed in Gurgi's close-set little eyes. "For the seeking of a piggy, there are many great lords in the forest, riding with frightening shouts. *They* would not be cruel to starving Gurgi – oh, no – they would feed him..."

"They would have your head off your shoulders before you could think twice about it," Gwydion said. "Did one of them wear an antlered mask?"

"Yes, yes!" Gurgi cried. "The great horns! You will save miserable Gurgi from hurtful choppings!" He set up a long and dreadful howling.

"I am losing patience with you," warned Gwydion. "Where is the pig?"

"Gurgi hears these mighty riders," the creature went on. "Oh, yes, with careful listenings from the trees. Gurgi is so quiet and clever, and no one cares about him. But he listens! These great warriors say they have gone to a certain place, but great fire turns them away. They are not pleased, and they will seek a piggy with outcries and horses."

"Gurgi," said Gwydion firmly, "where is the pig?"

"The piggy? Oh, terrible hunger pinches! Gurgi cannot remember. Was there a piggy? Gurgi is fainting and falling into the bushes, his poor, tender head is full of air from his empty belly."

Taran could no longer control his impatience. "Where is Hen Wen, you silly, hairy thing?" he burst out. "Tell us straight off! After the way you jumped on me, you deserve to have your head smacked."

With a moan, Gurgi rolled over on his back and covered his face with his arms.

Gwydion turned severely to Taran. "Had you followed my orders, you would not have been jumped on. Leave him to me. Do not make him any more frightened than he is." Gwydion looked down at Gurgi. "Very well," he asked calmly, "where is she?"

"Oh, fearful wrath!" Gurgi snuffled. "A piggy has gone across the water with swimmings and splashings." He sat upright and waved a woolly arm towards Great Avren.

"If you are lying to me," said Gwydion, "I shall soon find out. Then I will surely come back with wrath."

"Crunchings and munchings now, mighty prince?" said Gurgi in a high, tiny whimper.

"As I promised you," said Gwydion.

"Gurgi wants the smaller one for munchings," said the creature, with a beady glance at Taran.

"No, you do not," Gwydion said. "He is an Assistant Pig-Keeper and he would disagree with you violently." He unbuckled a saddlebag and pulled out a few strips of dried meat, which he tossed to Gurgi. "Be off now. Remember, I want no mischief from you."

Gurgi snatched the food, thrust it between his teeth, and scuttled up a tree trunk, leaping from tree to tree until he was out of sight.

"What a disgusting beast," said Taran. "What a nasty, vicious..."

"Oh, he is not bad at heart," Gwydion answered. "He would love to be wicked and terrifying, though he cannot quite manage it. He feels so sorry for himself that it is hard not to be angry with him. But there is no use in doing so."

"Was he telling the truth about Hen Wen?" asked Taran.

"I think he was," Gwydion said. "It is as I feared. The Horned King has ridden to Caer Dallben."

"He burned it!" Taran cried. Until now, he had paid little mind to his home. The thought of the white cottage in flames, his memory of Dallben's beard, and the heroic Coll's bald head touched him all at once. "Dallben and Coll are in peril!"

"Surely not," said Gwydion. "Dallben is an old fox. A beetle could not creep into Caer Dallben without his knowledge. No, I am certain the fire was something Dallben arranged for unexpected visitors.

"Hen Wen is the one in greatest peril. Our quest grows ever more urgent," Gwydion hastily continued. "The Horned King knows she is missing. He will pursue her."

"Then," Taran cried, "we must find her before he does!"

"Assistant Pig-Keeper," said Gwydion, "that has been, so far, your only sensible suggestion."

CHAPTER FOUR

The Gwythaints

Melyngar bore them swiftly through the fringe of trees lining Great Avren's sloping banks. They dismounted and hurried on foot in the direction Gurgi had indicated. Near a jagged rock, Gwydion halted and gave a cry of triumph. In a patch of clay, Hen Wen's tracks showed as plainly as if they had been carved.

"Good for Gurgi!" exclaimed Gwydion. "I hope he enjoys his crunchings and munchings! Had I known he would guide us so well, I would have given him an extra share.

41

"Yes, she crossed here," he went on, "and we shall do the same."

Gwydion led Melyngar forwards. The air had suddenly grown cold and heavy. The restless Avren ran grey, slashed with white streaks. Clutching Melyngar's saddle horn, Taran stepped gingerly from the bank.

Gwydion strode directly into the water. Taran, thinking it easier to get wet a little at a time, hung back as much as he could – until Melyngar lunged ahead, carrying him with her. His feet sought the river bottom, he stumbled and splashed, while icy waves swirled up to his neck. The current grew stronger, coiling like a grey serpent about Taran's legs. The bottom dropped away sharply; Taran lost his footing and found himself wildly dancing over nothing, as the river seized him greedily.

Melyngar began to swim, her strong legs keeping her afloat and in motion, but the current swung her around; she collided with Taran and forced him under the water.

"Let go the saddle!" Gwydion shouted above the torrent. "Swim clear of her!"

Water flooded Taran's ears and nostrils. With every gasp, the river poured into his lungs. Gwydion struck out after him, soon overtook him, seized him by the hair, and drew him towards the shallows. He heaved the dripping, coughing Taran onto the bank. Melyngar, reaching shore a little farther upstream, trotted down to join them.

Gwydion looked sharply at Taran. "I told you to swim clear. Are all Assistant Pig-Keepers deaf as well as stubborn?"

"I don't know how to swim!" Taran cried, his teeth chattering violently.

"Then why did you not say so before we started across?" Gwydion asked angrily.

"I was sure I could learn," Taran protested, "as soon as I came to do it. If Melyngar hadn't sat on me..."

"You must learn to answer for your own folly," said Gwydion. "As for Melyngar, she is wiser now than you can ever hope to become, even should you live to be a man — which seems more and more unlikely."

Gwydion swung into the saddle and pulled up the soaked, bedraggled Taran. Melyngar's hoofs clicked over the stones. Taran, snuffling and shivering, looked towards the waiting hills. High against the blue, three winged shapes wheeled and glided.

Gwydion, whose eyes were everywhere at once, caught sight of them instantly.

"Gwythaints!" he cried, and turned Melyngar sharply to the right. The abrupt change of direction and Melyngar's heaving burst of speed threw Taran off balance. His legs flew up and he landed flat on the pebble-strewn bank.

Gwydion reined in Melyngar immediately. While Taran

struggled to his feet, Gwydion seized him like a sack of meal and hauled him to Melyngar's back. The gwythaints, which, at a distance, had seemed no more than dry leaves in the wind, grew larger and larger, as they plunged towards horse and riders. Downwards they swooped, their great black wings driving them ever faster. Melyngar clattered up the riverbank. The gwythaints screamed above. At the line of trees, Gwydion thrust Taran from the saddle and leaped down. Dragging him along, Gwydion dropped to the earth under an oak tree's spreading branches.

The glittering wings beat against the foliage. Taran glimpsed curving beaks and talons merciless as daggers. He cried out in terror and hid his face, as the gwythaints veered off and swooped again. The leaves rattled in their wake. The creatures swung upwards, hung poised against the sky for an instant, then climbed swiftly and sped westwards.

White-faced and trembling, Taran ventured to raise his head. Gwydion strode to the riverbank and stood watching the gwythaints' flight. Taran made his way to his companion's side.

"I had hoped this would not happen," Gwydion said. His face was dark and grave. "Thus far, I have been able to avoid them."

Taran said nothing. He had clumsily fallen off Melyngar

at the moment when speed counted most; at the oak, he had behaved like a child. He waited for Gwydion's reprimand, but the warrior's green eyes followed the dark specks.

"Sooner or later they would have found us," Gwydion said. "They are Arawn's spies and messengers, the Eyes of Annuvin, they are called. No one stays long hidden from them. We are lucky they were only scouting and not on a blood hunt." He turned away as the gwythaints at last disappeared. "Now they fly to their iron cages in Annuvin," he said. "Arawn himself will have news of us before this day ends. He will not be idle."

"If only they hadn't seen us," Taran moaned.

"There is no use regretting what has happened," said Gwydion, as they set out again. "One way or another, Arawn would have learned of us. I have no doubt he knew the moment I rode from Caer Dathyl. The gwythaints are not his only servants."

"I think they must be the worst," said Taran, quickening his pace to keep up with Gwydion.

"Far from it," Gwydion said. "The errand of the gwythaints is less to kill than to bring information. For generations they have been trained in this. Arawn understands their language and they are in his power from the moment they leave the egg. Nevertheless, they are creatures of flesh and blood and a sword can answer them.

"There are others to whom a sword means nothing," Gwydion said. "Among them, the Cauldron Born, who serve Arawn as warriors."

"Are they not men?" Taran asked.

"They were, once," replied Gwydion. "They are the dead whose bodies Arawn steals from their resting places in the long barrows. It is said he steeps them in a cauldron to give them life again — if it can be called life. Like death, they are for ever silent; and their only thought is to bring others to the same bondage.

"Arawn keeps them as his guards in Annuvin, for their power wanes the longer and farther they be from their master. Yet from time to time Arawn sends certain of them outside Annuvin to perform his most ruthless tasks.

"These Cauldron Born are utterly without mercy or pity," Gwydion continued, "for Arawn has worked still greater evil upon them. He has destroyed their remembrance of themselves as living men. They have no memory of tears or laughter, of sorrow or loving kindness. Among all Arawn's deeds, this is one of the cruellest."

After much searching, Gwydion discovered Hen Wen's tracks once more. They led over a barren field, then to a shallow ravine.

"Here they stop," he said, frowning. "Even on stony ground there should be some trace, but I can see nothing."

Slowly and painstakingly he quartered the land on either side of the ravine. The weary and discouraged Taran could barely force himself to put one foot in front of the other, and was glad the dusk obliged Gwydion to halt.

Gwydion tethered Melyngar in a thicket. Taran sank to the ground and rested his head in his hands.

"She has disappeared too completely," said Gwydion, bringing provisions from the saddlebags. "Many things could have happened. Time is too short to ponder each one."

"What can we do, then?" Taran asked fearfully. "Is there no way to find her?"

"The surest search is not always the shortest," said Gwydion, "and we may need the help of other hands before it is done. There is an ancient dweller in the foothills of Eagle Mountains. His name is Medwyn, and it is said he understands the hearts and ways of every creature in Prydain. He, if anyone, should know where Hen Wen may be hiding."

"If we could find him," Taran began.

"You are right in saying 'if'," Gwydion answered. "I have never seen him. Others have sought him and failed. We should have only faint hope. But that is better than none at all."

A wind had risen, whispering among the black clusters

of trees. From a distance came the lonely baying of hounds. Gwydion sat upright, tense as a bowstring.

"Is it the Horned King?" cried Taran. "Has he followed us this closely?"

Gwydion shook his head. "No hounds bell like those, save the pack of Gwyn the Hunter. And so," he mused, "Gwyn, too, rides abroad."

"Another of Arawn's servants?" asked Taran, his voice betraying his anxiety.

"Gwyn owes allegiance to a lord unknown even to me," Gwydion answered, "and one perhaps greater than Arawn. Gwyn the Hunter rides alone with his dogs, and where he rides, slaughter follows. He has foreknowledge of death and battle, and watches from afar, marking the fall of warriors."

Above the cry of the pack rose the long, clear notes of a hunting horn. Flung across the sky, the sound pierced Taran's breast like a cold blade of terror. Yet, unlike the music itself, the echoes from the hills sang less of fear than of grief. Fading, they sighed that sunlight and birds, bright mornings, warm fires, food and drink, friendship, and all good things had been lost beyond recovery. Gwydion laid a firm hand on Taran's brow.

"Gwyn's music is a warning," Gwydion said. "Take it as a warning, for whatever profit that knowledge may be. But do not listen overmuch to the echoes. Others have done so, and have wandered hopeless ever since."

A whinny from Melyngar broke Taran's sleep. As Gwydion rose and went to her, Taran glimpsed a shadow dart behind a bush. He sat up quickly. Gwydion's back was turned. In the bright moonlight the shadow moved again. Choking back his fear, Taran leaped to his feet and plunged into the undergrowth. Thorns tore at him. He landed on something that grappled frantically. He lashed out, seized what felt like someone's head, and an unmistakable odour of wet wolfhound assailed his nose.

"Gurgi!" Taran cried furiously. "You sneaking..." The creature curled into an awkward ball as Taran began shaking him.

"Enough, enough!" Gwydion called. "Do not frighten the wits out of the poor thing!"

"Save your own life next time!" Taran retorted angrily to Gwydion, while Gurgi began howling at the top of his voice. "I should have known a great war-leader needs no help from an Assistant Pig-Keeper!"

"Unlike Assistant Pig-Keepers," Gwydion said gently, "I scorn the help of no man. And you should know better than to jump into thornbushes without first making sure what you will find. Save your anger for a better purpose..." He hesitated and looked carefully at Taran. "Why, I believe you did think my life was in danger."

"If I had known it was only that stupid, silly Gurgi..."

"The fact is, you did not," Gwydion said. "So I shall take the intention for the deed. You may be many other things, Taran of Caer Dallben, but I see you are no coward. I offer you my thanks," he added, bowing deeply.

"And what of poor Gurgi?" howled the creature. "No thanks for him – oh, no – only smackings by great lords! Not even a small munching for helping find a piggy!"

"We didn't find any piggy," Taran replied angrily. "And if you ask me, you know too much about the Horned King. I wouldn't be surprised if you'd gone and told him..."

"No, no! The lord of the great horns pursues wise, miserable Gurgi with leaping and galloping. Gurgi fears terrible smackings and whackings. He follows kindly and mighty protectors. Faithful Gurgi will not leave them, never!"

"And what of the Horned King?" Gwydion asked quickly.

"Oh, very angry," whined Gurgi. "Wicked lords ride with mumblings and grumblings because they cannot find a piggy."

"Where are they now?" asked Gwydion.

"Not far. They cross water, but only clever, unthanked Gurgi knows where. And they light fires with fearsome blazings."

"Can you lead us to them?" Gwydion asked. "I would learn their plans."

Gurgi whimpered questioningly. "Crunchings and munchings?"

"I knew he would get round to that," said Taran.

Gwydion saddled Melyngar and, clinging to the shadows, they set out across the moonlit hills. Gurgi led the way, loping ahead, bent forwards, his long arms dangling. They crossed one deep valley, then another, before Gurgi halted on a ridge. Below, the wide plain blazed with torches and Taran saw a great ring of flames.

"Crunchings and munchings now?" Gurgi suggested.

Disregarding him, Gwydion motioned for them all to descend the slope. There was little need for silence. A deep, hollow drumming throbbed over the crowded plain. Horses whickered; there came the shouts of men and the clank of weapons. Gwydion crouched in the bracken, watching intently. Around the fiery circle, warriors on high stilts beat upraised swords against their shields.

"What are those men?" Taran whispered. "And the wicker baskets hanging from the posts?"

"They are the Proud Walkers," Gwydion answered, "in a dance of battle, an ancient rite of war from the days when men were no more than savages. The baskets – another ancient custom best forgotten.

"But look there!" Gwydion cried suddenly. "The

Horned King! And there," he exclaimed, pointing to the columns of horsemen, "I see the banners of the Cantrev Rheged! The banners of Dau Gleddyn and Mawr! All the cantrevs of the south! Yes, now I understand!"

Before Gwydion could speak again, the Horned King, bearing a torch, rode to the wicker baskets and thrust the fire into them. Flames seized the osier cages; billows of foul smoke rose skywards. The warriors clashed their shields and shouted together with one voice. From the baskets rose the agonized screams of men. Taran gasped and turned away.

"We have seen enough," Gwydion ordered. "Hurry, let us be gone from here."

Dawn had broken when Gwydion halted at the edge of the barren field. Until now, he had not spoken. Even Gurgi had been silent, his eyes round with terror.

"This is a part of what I have journeyed so far to learn," Gwydion said. His face was grim and pale. "Arawn now dares try force of arms, with the Horned King as his war-leader. The Horned King has raised a mighty host, and they will march against us. The Sons of Don are ill prepared for so powerful an enemy. They must be warned. I must return to Caer Dathyl immediately."

From a corner of woodland, five mounted warriors cantered into the field. Taran sprang up. The first horseman spurred his mount to a gallop. Melyngar whinnied shrilly. The warriors drew their swords.

CHAPTER FIVE

The Broken Sword

Gurgi ran off, yelping in terror. Gwydion was at Taran's side as the first rider bore down on them. With a quick gesture, Gwydion thrust a hand into his jacket and pulled out the net of grass. Suddenly the withered wisps grew larger, longer, shimmering and crackling, nearly blinding Taran with streaks of liquid flame. The rider raised the sword. With a shout, Gwydion hurled the dazzling mesh into the warrior's face. Shrieking, the rider dropped his sword and grappled the air. He tumbled from his saddle while the mesh spread over his body and clung to him like an enormous spiderweb.

Gwydion dragged the stupefied Taran to an ash tree and from his belt drew the hunting knife which he thrust in Taran's hand. "This is the only weapon I can spare," he cried. "Use it as well as you can."

His back to the tree, Gwydion faced the four remaining warriors. The great sword swung a glittering arc, the flashing blade sang above Gwydion's head. The attackers drove against them. One horse reared. For Taran there was only a vision of hoofs plunging at his face. The rider chopped viciously at Taran's head, swung around, and struck again. Blindly, Taran lashed out with the knife. Shouting in rage and pain, the rider clutched his leg and wheeled his horse away.

There was no sign of Gurgi, but a white streak sped across the field. Melyngar now had entered the fray. Her golden mane tossing, the white mare whinnied fearsomely and flung herself among the riders. Her mighty flanks dashed against them, crowding, pressing, while the steeds of the war party rolled their eyes in panic. One warrior jerked frantically at his reins to turn his mount away. The animal sank to its haunches. Melyngar reared to her full height; her forelegs churned the air, and her sharp hoofs slashed at the rider, who fell heavily to earth. Melyngar spun about, trampling the cowering horseman.

The three mounted warriors forced their way past the frenzied mare. At the ash tree, Gwydion's blade rang and clashed among the leaves. His legs were as though planted in the earth; the shock of the galloping riders could not dislodge him. His eyes shone with a terrible light.

"Hold your ground but a little while," he called to Taran. The sword whistled, one rider gave a choking cry. The other two did not press the attack, but hung back for a moment.

Hoofbeats pounded over the meadow. Even as the attackers had begun to withdraw, two more riders galloped forwards. They reined their horses sharply, dismounted without hesitation, and ran swiftly towards Gwydion. Their faces were pallid; their eyes like stones. Heavy bands of bronze circled their waists, and from these belts hung the black thongs of whips. Knobs of bronze studded their breastplates. They did not bear shield or helmet. Their mouths were frozen in the hideous grin of death.

Gwydion's sword flashed up once more. "Fly!" he cried to Taran. "These are the Cauldron‚Born! Take Melyngar and ride from here!"

Taran set himself more firmly against the ash tree and raised his knife. In another instant, the Cauldron‚Born were upon them.

For Taran, the horror beating in him like black wings came not from the livid features of the Cauldron warriors or their lightless eyes but from their ghostly silence. The mute men swung their swords, metal grated against metal. The relentless warriors struck and struck again. Gwydion's blade leaped past one opponent's guard and drove deep into his heart. The pale warrior made no outcry. No blood followed as Gwydion ripped the weapon free; the Cauldron-Born shook himself once, without a grimace, and moved again to the attack.

Gwydion stood as a wolf at bay, his green eyes glittering, his teeth bared. The swords of the Cauldron-Born beat against his guard. Taran thrust at one of the livid warriors; a sword point ripped his arm and sent the small knife hurtling into the bracken.

Blood streaked Gwydion's face where an unlucky blow had slashed his cheekbone and forehead. Once, his blade faltered and a Cauldron-Born thrust at his breast. Gwydion turned, taking the sword point in his side. The pale warriors doubled their assault.

The great shaggy head bowed wearily as Gwydion stumbled forwards. With a mighty cry, he lunged, then dropped to one knee. With his flagging strength, he fought to raise the blade again. The Cauldron-Born flung aside their weapons, seized him, threw him to the ground, and quickly bound him.

Now the other two warriors approached. One grasped Taran by the throat, the other tied his hands behind him.

Taran was dragged to Melyngar and thrown across her back, where he lay side by side with Gwydion.

"Are you badly hurt?" asked Gwydion, striving to raise his head.

"No," Taran said, "but your own wound is grave."

"It is not the wound that pains me," said Gwydion with a bitter smile. "I have taken worse and lived. Why did you not flee, as I ordered? I knew I was powerless against the Cauldron-Born, but I could have held the ground for you. Yet, you fought well enough, Taran of Caer Dallben."

"You are more than a war-leader," Taran whispered. "Why do you keep the truth from me? I remember the net of grass you wove before we crossed Avren. But in your hands today it was no grass I have ever seen."

"I am what I told you. The wisp of grass – yes, it is a little more than that. Dallben himself taught me the use of it."

"You, too, are an enchanter!"

"I have certain skills. Alas, they are not great enough to defend myself against the powers of Arawn. Today," he added, "they were not enough to protect a brave companion."

One of the Cauldron-Born spurred his horse alongside Melyngar. Snatching the whip from his belt, he lashed brutally at the captives.

"Say no more," Gwydion whispered. "You will only bring yourself pain. If we should not meet again, farewell."

The party rode along without a halt. Fording the shallow River Ystrad, the Cauldron-Born pressed tightly on either side of the captives. Taran dared once again to speak to Gwydion, but the lash cut his words short. Taran's throat was parched, waves of dizziness threatened to drown him. He could not be sure how long they had ridden, for he lapsed often into feverish dreams. The sun was still high and he was dimly aware of a hill with a tall, grey fortress looming at its crest. Melyngar's hoofs rang on stones as a courtyard opened before him. Rough hands pulled him from Melyngar's back and drove him, stumbling, down an arching corridor. Gwydion was half-dragged, half-carried before him. Taran tried to catch up with his companion, but the lash of the Cauldron-Born beat him to his knees. A guard hauled him upright again and kicked him forwards.

At length, the captives were led into a spacious council chamber. Torches flickered from walls hung with scarlet tapestries. Outside, it had been full daylight; here in the great, windowless hall, the chill and dampness of night rose from the cold flagstones like mist. At the far end of the hall, on a throne carved of black wood, sat a woman. Her long hair glittered silver in the torchlight. Her face was young and beautiful; her pale skin seemed paler still above her crimson robe. Jewelled necklaces hung at her throat, gem-studded bracelets circled her wrists, and heavy rings threw back the flickering torches. Gwydion's sword lay at her feet.

The woman rose quickly. "What shame to my household is this?" she cried at the warriors. "The wounds of these men are fresh and untended. Someone shall answer for this neglect!" She stopped in front of Taran. "And this lad can barely keep his feet." She clapped her hands. "Bring food and wine and medicine for their injuries."

She turned again to Taran. "Poor boy," she said, with a pitying smile, "there has been grievous mischief done today." She touched his wound with a soft, pale hand. At the pressure of her fingers, a comforting warmth filled Taran's aching body. Instead of pain, a delicious sensation of repose came over him, repose as he remembered it from days long forgotten in Caer Dallben, the warm bed of his childhood, drowsy summer afternoons. "How do you come here?" she asked quietly.

"We crossed Great Avren," Taran began. "You see, what had happened..."

"Silence!" Gwydion's voice rang out. "She is Achren! She sets a trap for you!"

Taran gasped. For an instant he could not believe such beauty concealed the evil of which he had been warned. Had Gwydion mistaken her? Nevertheless, he shut his lips tightly.

The woman, in surprise, turned to Gwydion. "This is not courtesy to accuse me thus. Your wound excuses your conduct, but there is no need for anger. Who are you? Why do you..."

Gwydion's eyes flashed. "You know me as well as I know you, Achren!" He spat the name through his bleeding lips.

"I have heard Lord Gwydion was travelling in my realm. Beyond that..."

"Arawn sent his warriors to slay us," cried Gwydion, "and here they stand in your council hall. Do you say that you know nothing more?"

"Arawn sent warriors to find, not slay you," answered Achren, "or you would not be alive at this moment. Now that I see you face to face," she said, her eyes on Gwydion, "I am glad such a man is not bleeding out his life in a ditch. For there is much we have to discuss, and much that you can profit from."

"If you would treat with me," said Gwydion, "unbind me and return my sword."

"You make demands?" Achren asked gently. "Perhaps you do not understand. I offer you something you cannot have even if I loosened your hands and gave back your weapon. By that, Lord Gwydion, I mean — your life."

"In exchange for what?"

"I had thought to bargain with another life," said Achren, glancing at Taran. "But I see he is of no consequence, alive or dead. No," she said, "there are other, pleasanter ways to bargain. You do not know me as well as you think, Gwydion. There is no future for you beyond these gates. Here, I can promise..."

"Your promises reek of Annuvin!" cried Gwydion. "I scorn them. It is no secret what you are!"

Achren's face turned livid. Hissing, she struck at Gwydion and her blood-red nails raked his cheek. Achren unsheathed Gwydion's sword; holding it in both hands she drove the point towards his throat, stopping only a hairbreadth from it. Gwydion stood proudly, his eyes blazing.

"No," cried Achren, "I will not slay you; you shall come to wish I had, and beg the mercy of a sword! You scorn my promises! This promise will be well kept!"

Achren raised the sword above her head and smote with all her force against a stone pillar. Sparks flashed, the blade rang unbroken. With a scream of rage, she dashed the weapon to the ground.

The sword shone, still undamaged. Achren seized it again, gripping the sharp blade itself until her hands ran scarlet. Her eyes rolled back into her head, her lips moved and twisted. A thunderclap filled the hall, a light burst like a crimson sun, and the broken weapon fell in pieces to the ground.

"So shall I break you!" Achren shrieked. She raised

her hand to the Cauldron-Born and called out in a strange, harsh language.

The pale warriors strode forwards and dragged Taran and Gwydion from the hall. In a dark passageway of stone, Taran struggled with his captors, fighting to reach Gwydion's side. One of the Cauldron-Born brought a whip handle down on Taran's head.

CHAPTER SIX

Eilonwy

Taran came to his senses on a pile of dirty straw, which smelled as though Gurgi and all his ancestors had slept on it. A few feet above him, pale yellow sunlight shone through a grating; the feeble beam ended abruptly on a wall of rough, damp stone. The shadows of bars lay across the tiny patch of light; instead of brightening the cell, the wan rays made it appear only more grim and closed in. As Taran's eyes grew accustomed to this yellow twilight, he made out a heavy, studded portal with a slot at the base. The cell itself was no more than three paces square.

His head ached; since his hands were still bound behind him, he could do no more than guess at the large and throbbing lump. What had happened to Gwydion he dared not imagine. After the Cauldron warrior had struck him, Taran had regained consciousness only a few moments before slipping once again into whirling darkness. In that brief time, he vaguely remembered opening his eyes and finding himself slung over a guard's back. His confused recollection included a dim corridor with doors on either side. Gwydion had called out to him once – or so Taran believed – he could not recall his friend's words, perhaps even that had been part of the nightmare. He supposed Gwydion had been cast in another dungeon; Taran fervently hoped so. He could not shake off the memory of Achren's livid face and horrible screaming, and he feared she might have ordered Gwydion slain.

Still, there was good reason to hope his companion lived. Achren could easily have cut his throat as he braved her in the council hall, yet she had held back. Thus, she intended to keep Gwydion alive; perhaps, Taran thought wretchedly, Gwydion would be better off dead. The idea of the proud figure lying a broken corpse filled Taran with grief that quickly turned to rage. He staggered to his feet, lurched to the door, kicking it, battering himself against it with what little strength remained to him. In despair, he sank to the damp ground, his head pressed against the unyielding oaken planks. He rose again after a few moments and kicked at the walls. If Gwydion were, by chance, in an adjoining cell, Taran hoped he would hear this signal. But he judged, from the dull and muffled sound, that the walls were too thick for his feeble tapping to penetrate.

As he turned away, a flashing object fell through the grating and dropped to the stone floor. Taran stooped. It was a ball of what seemed to be gold. Perplexed, he looked upwards. From the grating, a pair of intensely blue eyes looked back at him.

"Please," said a girl's voice, light and musical, "my name is Eilonwy and if you don't mind, would you throw my bauble to me? I don't want you to think I'm a baby, playing with a silly bauble, because I'm not; but sometimes there's absolutely nothing else to do around here and it slipped out of my hands when I was tossing it..."

"Little girl," Taran interrupted, "I don't..."

"But I am not a little girl," Eilonwy protested. "Haven't I just been and finished telling you? Are you slow-witted? I'm so sorry for you. It's terrible to be dull and stupid. What's your name?" she went on. "It makes me feel funny not knowing someone's name. Wrong-footed, you know, or as if I had three thumbs on one hand, if you see what I mean. It's clumsy..."

"I am Taran of Caer Dallben," Taran said, then wished

he had not. This, he realized, could be another trap.

"That's lovely," Eilonwy said gaily. "I'm very glad to meet you. I suppose you're a lord, or a warrior, or a war-leader, or a bard, or a monster. Though we haven't had any monsters for a long time."

"I am none of those," said Taran, feeling quite flattered that Eilonwy should have taken him for any one of them.

"What else is there?"

"I am an Assistant Pig-Keeper," Taran said. He bit his lip as soon as the words were out; then, to excuse his loose tongue, told himself it could do no harm for the girl to know that much.

"How fascinating," Eilonwy said. "You're the first we've ever had — unless that poor fellow in the other dungeon is one, too."

"Tell me of him," Taran said quickly. "Is he alive?"

"I don't know," said Eilonwy. "I peeked through the grating, but I couldn't tell. He doesn't move at all, but I should imagine he is alive; otherwise, Achren would have fed him to the ravens. Now, please, if you don't mind, it's right at your feet."

"I can't pick up your bauble," Taran said, "because my hands are tied."

The blue eyes looked surprised. "Oh? Well, that would account for it. Then I suppose I shall have to come in and get it."

"You can't come in and get it," said Taran wearily. "Don't you see I'm locked up here?"

"Of course I do," said Eilonwy. "What would be the point of having someone in a dungeon if they weren't locked up? Really, Taran of Caer Dallben, you surprise me with some of your remarks. I don't mean to hurt your feelings by asking, but is Assistant Pig-Keeper the kind of work that calls for a great deal of intelligence?"

Something beyond the grating and out of Taran's vision swooped down and the blue eyes disappeared suddenly. Taran heard what he took to be a scuffle, then a high-pitched little shriek, followed by a larger shriek and a moment or two of loud smacking.

The blue eyes did not reappear. Taran flung himself back on the straw. After a time, in the dreadful silence and loneliness of the tiny cell, he began suddenly to wish Eilonwy would come back. She was the most confusing person he had ever met, and surely as wicked as everyone else in the castle – although he could not quite bring himself to believe it completely. Nevertheless, he longed for the sound of another voice, even Eilonwy's prattling.

The grating above his head darkened. Night poured into the cell in a black, chilly wave. The slot in the heavy portal rattled open. Taran heard something being slid into the cell and crawled towards it. It was a shallow bowl. He sniffed carefully and finally ventured to touch his tongue to it, fearing all the while that it might be poisoned food. It was not food at all, but only a little water, warm and musty. His throat was so parched that Taran disregarded the taste, thrust his face into the bowl, and drank it dry.

He curled up and tried to sleep away his pain; the tight thongs pinched, but his swollen hands were mercifully numb. Sleep brought only nightmares and he roused to find himself shouting aloud. He settled down once more. Now there was a rasping sound under the straw.

Taran stumbled to his feet. The rasping grew louder.

"Move away!" cried a faint voice.

Taran looked around him, dumbfounded.

"Get off the stone!"

He stepped backwards. The voice was coming from the straw.

"Well, I can't lift it with you standing on it, you silly Assistant Pig-Keeper!" the muffled voice complained.

Frightened and puzzled, Taran jumped to the wall. The pallet began rising upwards. A loose flagstone was lifted, pushed aside, and a slender shadow emerged as if from the ground itself.

"Who are you?" Taran shouted.

"Who did you expect?" said the voice of Eilonwy. "And please don't make such a racket. I told you I was coming back. Oh, there's my bauble..." The shadow bent and picked up the luminous ball.

"Where are you?" cried Taran. "I can see nothing..."

"Is that what's bothering you?" Eilonwy asked. "Why didn't you say so in the first place?" Instantly, a bright light filled the cell. It came from the golden sphere in the girl's hand.

Taran blinked with amazement. "What's that?" he cried.

"It's my bauble," said Eilonwy. "How many times do I have to tell you?"

"But — but it lights up!"

"What did you think it would do? Turn into a bird and fly away?"

Eilonwy, as the bewildered Taran saw her for the first time, had, in addition to blue eyes, long hair of reddish gold reaching to her waist. Her face, though smudged, was delicate, elfin, with high cheekbones. Her short, white robe, mud-stained, was girdled with silver links. A crescent moon of silver hung from a fine chain around her neck. She was one or two years younger than he, but fully as tall. Eilonwy put the glowing sphere on the floor, went quickly to Taran, and unknotted the thongs that bound him.

"I meant to come back sooner," Eilonwy said. "But Achren caught me talking to you. She started to give me a whipping. I bit her.

"Then she locked me in one of the chambers, deep underground," Eilonwy went on, pointing to the flagstones. "There are hundreds of them under Spiral Castle, and all kinds of galleries and little passages, like a honeycomb. Achren didn't build them; this castle, they say, once belonged to a great king. She thinks she knows all the passageways. But she doesn't. She hasn't been in half of them. Can you imagine Achren going through a tunnel? She's older than she looks, you know." Eilonwy giggled. "But I know every one, and most of them connect with each other. It took me longer in the dark, though, because I didn't have my bauble."

"You mean you live in this terrible place?" Taran asked.

"Naturally," Eilonwy said. "You don't imagine I'd want to visit here, do you?"

"Is – is Achren your mother?" Taran gasped and drew back fearfully.

"Certainly not!" cried the girl. "I am Eilonwy Daughter of Angharad, Daughter of Regat Daughter of – oh, it's such a bother going through all that. My ancestors," she said proudly, "are the Sea People. I am of the blood of Llyr Half-Speech, the Sea King. Achren is my aunt, though sometimes I don't think she's really my aunt at all."

"Then what are you doing here?"

"I said I live here," Eilonwy answered. "It must take a lot of explaining before you understand anything. My parents died and my kinsmen sent me here so Achren could teach me to be an enchantress. It's a family tradition, don't

71

you see? The boys are war-leaders, and the girls are enchantresses."

"Achren is leagued with Arawn of Annuvin," cried Taran. "She is an evil, loathsome creature!"

"Oh, everybody knows that," said Eilonwy. "Sometimes I wish my kinsmen had sent me to someone else. But I think they must have forgotten about me by now."

She noticed a deep slash on his arm. "Where did you get that?" she asked. "I don't think you know much about fighting if you let yourself get knocked about and cut up so badly. But I don't imagine Assistant Pig-Keepers are often called on to do that sort of thing." The girl tore a strip from the hem of her robe and began binding Taran's wound.

"I didn't *let* myself be cut up," Taran said angrily. "That's Arawn's doing, or your aunt's – I don't know which and I don't care. One is no better than the other."

"I hate Achren!" Eilonwy burst out. "She is a mean, spiteful person. Of all the people who come here, you're the only one who's the least bit agreeable to talk to – and she had you damaged!"

"That's not the end of it," Taran said. "She means to kill my friend."

"If she does that," said Eilonwy, "I'm sure she'll include you. Achren doesn't do things by halves. It would be a shame if you were killed. I should be very sorry. I know I wouldn't like it to happen to me..."

"Eilonwy, listen," Taran interrupted, "if there are tunnels and passages under the castle – can you get to the other cells? Is there a way outside?"

"Of course there is," Eilonwy said. "If there's a way in, there has to be a way out, doesn't there?"

"Will you help us?" Taran asked. "It is important for us to be free of this place. Will you show us the passage?"

"Let you escape?" Eilonwy giggled. "Wouldn't Achren be furious at that!" She tossed her head. "It would serve her right for whipping me and trying to lock me up. Yes, yes," she went on, her eyes dancing, "that's a wonderful idea. I would love to see her face when she comes down to find you. Yes, that would be more fun than anything I could think of. Can you imagine..."

"Listen carefully," Taran said, "is there a way you can take me to my companion?"

Eilonwy shook her head. "That would be very hard to do. You see, some of the galleries connect with the ones leading to the cells, but when you try to go across, what happens is that you start to run into passages that..."

"Never mind, then," Taran said. " Can I join him in one of the passageways?"

"I don't see why you want to do that," said the girl. "It would be so much simpler if I just go and let him out and have him wait for you beyond the castle. I don't understand why you want to complicate things; it's bad enough for two people crawling about, but with three, you can imagine what that would be. And you can't possibly find your way by yourself."

"Very well," Taran said impatiently. "Free my companion first. I only hope he is well enough to move. If he isn't, then you must come and tell me right away and I'll think of some means of carrying him.

"And there is a white horse, Melyngar," Taran went on. "I don't know what's been done with her."

"She would be in the stable," Eilonwy said. "Isn't that where you'd usually find a horse?"

"Please," Taran said, "you must get her, too. And weapons for us. Will you do that?"

Eilonwy nodded quickly. "Yes, that should be very exciting." She giggled again. She picked up the glowing ball, cupped it in her hands, and once again the cell was dark. The stone grated shut and only Eilonwy's silvery laugh lingered behind.

Taran paced back and forth. For the first time, he felt some hope; though he wondered how much he could count on this scatterbrained girl. She was likely to forget what she started out to do. Worse, she might betray him to Achren. It might be another trap, a new torment that promised him freedom only to snatch it away, but even so, Taran decided, they could be no worse off.

To save his energy, he lay down on the straw and tried

to relax. His bandaged arm no longer pained him, and while he was still hungry and thirsty, the water he had drunk had taken some of the edge from his discomfort.

He had no idea how long it would take to travel through the underground galleries. But as time passed, he grew more anxious. He worked at the flagstone the girl had used. It would not move, though Taran's efforts bloodied his fingers. He sank again into dark, endless waiting. Eilonwy did not return.

CHAPTER SEVEN

The Trap

From the corridor, a faint sound grew louder. Taran hastened to press his ear against the slot in the portal. He heard the heavy tread of marching feet, the rattle of weapons. He straightened and stood with his back to the wall. The girl had betrayed him. He cast about for some means to defend himself, for he had determined they would not take him easily. For the sake of having something in his hands, Taran picked up the dirty straw and held it ready to fling; it was a pitiable defence, and he wished desperately for Gwydion's power to set it ablaze.

The footsteps continued. He feared, then, they would enter the other cell. He breathed a sigh of relief when they did not stop but faded away towards what he imagined to be the far end of the corridor. Perhaps the guard was being changed.

He turned away, certain Eilonwy would not be back, and furious with her and her false promises. She was a rattlebrained fool who would undoubtedly giggle and take it as a great joke when the Cauldron-Born came for him. He buried his face in his hands. He could hear her chatter even now. Taran started up again. The voice he heard was real.

"Must you always sit on the wrong stone?" it said. "You're too heavy to lift."

Taran jumped up and hurriedly cleared the straw away. The flagstone was raised. The light from the golden ball was dim now, but enough for him to see that Eilonwy looked pleased with herself.

"Your companion is free," she whispered. "And I took Melyngar from the stable. They are hidden in the woods outside the castle. It's all done now," Eilonwy said gleefully. "They're waiting for you. So if you get a move on and stop looking as if you'd forgotten your own name, we can go and meet them."

"Did you find weapons?" Taran asked.

"Well, no. I didn't have a chance to look," Eilonwy said. "Really," she added, "you can't expect me to do everything, can you?"

Eilonwy held the glowing sphere close to the stone floor. "Go first," she said. "Then I'll come down after, so I can put the stone back in place. Then, when Achren sends to have you killed, there won't be any trace at all. She'll think you disappeared into thin air – and that will make it all the more vexing. I know it isn't nice to vex people on purpose – it's like handing them a toad – but this is much too good to miss and I may never have another chance at it."

"Achren will know you let us escape," Taran said.

"No, she won't," said Eilonwy, "because she'll think I'm still locked up. And if she doesn't know I can get out, she can't know I was here. But it's very thoughtful of you to say that. It shows a kind heart, and I think that's so much more important than being clever."

While Eilonwy continued to chatter away, Taran lowered himself into the narrow opening. The passage was low, he discovered, and he was obliged to crouch almost on hands and knees.

Eilonwy moved the stone into place and then began to lead the way. The glow from the sphere showed walls of hard-packed earth. As Taran hunched along, other galleries opened up on either side.

"Be sure you follow me," Eilonwy called. "Don't go into any of those. Some of them branch off and some of them don't go anywhere at all. You'd get lost, and that would be a useless thing to do if you're trying to escape."

The girl moved so quickly Taran had difficulty keeping up with her. Twice he stumbled over loose stones in the passage, clutched at the ground, and pitched forwards. The little light bobbed ahead, while behind him long fingers of darkness grasped his heels. He could understand why Achren's fortress was called Spiral Castle. The narrow, stifling galleries turned endlessly; he could not be sure whether they were making real progress or whether the tunnel was merely doubling back on itself.

The earthen ceiling trembled with racing footsteps.

"We're just below the guardroom," Eilonwy whispered. "Something's happening up there. Achren doesn't usually turn out the guard in the middle of the night."

"They must have gone to the cells," Taran said. "There was a lot of commotion just before you came. They surely know we're gone."

"You must be a very important Assistant Pig-Keeper," said Eilonwy with a small laugh. "Achren wouldn't go to all that trouble unless..."

"Hurry," Taran urged. "If she puts a guard around the castle we'll never get out."

"I wish you'd stop worrying," Eilonwy said. "You sound

as if you were having your toes twisted. Achren can set out all the guards she wants. She doesn't know where the mouth of the tunnel is. And it's hidden so well an owl couldn't see it. After all, you don't think I'd march you out the front gate, do you?"

Despite her chattering, Eilonwy kept a rapid pace. Taran bent close to the ground, moving half by touch, keeping his eyes on the faint glow; he skidded past sharp turns, fetched up against rough walls, skinned his knees, then had to move twice as fast to regain the ground he had lost. At another bend in the passageway, Eilonwy's light wavered and dropped out of sight. In the moment of darkness, Taran lost his footing as the ground rose steeply on one side. He fell and rolled. Before he could recover his balance, he was sliding rapidly downwards in a shower of loose stones and earth. He collided with an outcropping of rock, rolled again, and dropped suddenly into the darkness.

He landed heavily on flat stones, legs twisted under him. Taran climbed painfully to his feet and shook his head to clear it. Suddenly he realized he was standing upright. Eilonwy and her light could not be seen. He called as loudly as he dared.

After a few moments he heard a scraping above him and saw the faint reflection of the golden ball. "Where are you?" called the girl. Her voice seemed quite distant. "Oh

– I see. Part of the tunnel's given way. You must have slipped into a crevice."

"It's not a crevice," Taran called. "I've fallen all the way down into something and it's deep. Can't you put the light into it? I've got to get up again."

There were more scraping noises. "Yes," Eilonwy said, "you have got yourself into a mess. The ground's all broken through here, and below there's a big stone, like a shelf over your head. How *did* you ever manage to do that?"

"I don't know how," replied Taran, "but I certainly didn't do it on purpose."

"It's strange," Eilonwy said. "This wasn't here when I came through the first time. All that tramping must have jarred something loose; it's hard to say. I don't think these tunnels are half as solid as they look, and neither is the castle, for the matter of that; Achren's always complaining about things leaking and doors not closing right..."

"Do stop that prattling," cried Taran, clasping his head. "I don't want to hear about leaks and doors. Show a light so I can climb out of here."

"That's the trouble," the girl said. "I'm not quite sure you can. You see, that shelf of stone juts out so far and goes down so steeply. Can you manage to reach it?"

Taran raised his arms and jumped as high as he could. He could find no handhold. From Eilonwy's description, and from the massive shadow above, he feared the girl was right. He could not reach the stone and, even if he could have, its sharp downward pitch would have made it impossible to climb. Taran groaned with despair.

"Go on without me," he said. "Warn my companion the castle is alerted..."

"And what do you intend doing? You can't just sit there like a fly in a jug. That isn't going to help matters at all."

"It doesn't make any difference about me," Taran said. "You can find a rope and come back when things are safe..."

"Who knows when that will be? If Achren sees me, there's no telling what might happen. And suppose I couldn't get back? You'd turn into a skeleton while you're waiting – I don't know how long it takes for people to turn into skeletons, though I imagine it would need some time – and you'd be worse off than before."

"What else am I to do?" cried Taran.

Eilonwy's talk of skeletons made his blood run cold. He recalled, then, the sound of Gwyn the Hunter's horn and the memory of it filled him with grief and fear. He bowed his head and turned his face to the rough wall.

"That's very noble of you," said Eilonwy, "but I don't think it's really necessary, not yet, at any rate. If Achren's warriors come out and start beating the woods, I hardly think your friend would stay around waiting. He'd go and hide and find you later, or so I should imagine. That would be the sensible thing to do. Of course, if he's an Assistant

Pig Keeper, too, it's hard to guess how his mind would work."

"He's not an Assistant Pig Keeper," Taran said. "He's… well, it's none of your business what he is."

"That's not a very polite thing to say. Well, nevertheless…" Eilonwy's voice dismissed the matter. "The main thing is to get you out."

"There's nothing we can do," Taran said. "I'm caught here, and locked up better than Achren ever planned."

"Don't say that. I could tear up my robe and plait it into a cord – though I'll tell you right away I wouldn't enjoy crawling around tunnels without any clothes on. But I don't think it would be long enough or strong enough. I suppose I could cut off my hair, if I had a pair of shears, and add it in – no, that still wouldn't do. Won't you please be quiet for a while and let me think? Wait, I'm going to drop my bauble down to you. Here, catch!"

The golden sphere came hurtling over the ledge. Taran caught it in mid air.

"Now then," Eilonwy called, "what's down there? Is it just a pit of some kind?"

Taran raised the ball above his head. "Why, it's not a hole at all!" he cried. "It's a kind of chamber. There's a tunnel here, too." He took a few paces. "I can't see where it ends. It's big…"

Stones rattled behind him; an instant later, Eilonwy dropped to the ground. Taran stared at her in disbelief.

"You fool!" he shouted. "You addlepated... What have you done? Now both of us are trapped! And you talk about sense! You haven't..."

Eilonwy smiled at him and waited until he ran out of breath. "Now," she said, "if you've quite finished, let me explain something very simple to you. If there's a tunnel, it has to go someplace. And wherever it goes, there's a very good chance it will be better than where we are now."

"I didn't mean to call you names," Taran said, "but," he added sorrowfully, "there was no reason for you to put yourself in danger."

"There you go again," Eilonwy said. "I promised to help you escape and that's what I'm doing. I understand about tunnels and I shouldn't be surprised if this one followed the same direction as the one above. It doesn't have half as many galleries coming off it. And, besides, it's a lot more comfortable."

Eilonwy took the glowing sphere from Taran's hand and stepped forwards into the new passageway. Still doubtful, Taran followed.

CHAPTER EIGHT

The Barrow

As Eilonwy had said, the passageway was more comfortable, for they could walk side by side without crouching and scuttling like rabbits in a warren. Unlike those of the upper galleries, the walls were lined with huge, flat stones; the ceiling was formed of even larger stones, whose weight was supported by upright slabs set at intervals along the square corridor. The air, too, smelled slightly better; musty, as if it had lain unstirred for ages, but without the choking closeness of the tunnels.

None of this comforted Taran greatly. Eilonwy herself admitted she had never explored the passage; her blithe confidence did not convince him she had the slightest notion of where she was going. Nevertheless, the girl hurried along, her sandals tapping and echoing, the golden light of the bauble casting its rays through shadows that hung like cobwebs.

They passed a few side galleries which Eilonwy ignored. "We'll go straight to the end of this one," she announced. "There's bound to be something there."

Taran had begun wishing himself back in the chamber. "We shouldn't have come this far," he said, with a frown. "We should have stayed and found some way to climb out; now you don't even know how long it will be before this passage stops. We might go on tramping for days."

Something else troubled him. After all their progress, it seemed the passageway should now follow an upwards direction.

"The tunnel's supposed to bring us out above ground," Taran said. "But we haven't stopped going down. We aren't coming out at all; we're only going deeper and deeper."

Eilonwy paid no attention to his remarks.

But she was soon obliged to. Within another few paces, the corridor stopped abruptly, sealed by a wall of boulders.

"This is what I feared," cried Taran, dismayed. "We have gone to the end of your tunnel, that you know so much about, and this is what we find. Now we can only go back; we've lost all our time and we're no better off than when we started." He turned away while the girl stood looking curiously at the barrier.

"I can't understand," said Eilonwy, "why anyone would go to the trouble of building a tunnel and not have it go anyplace. It must have been a terrible amount of work for whoever it was to dig it all and set in the rocks. Why do you suppose...?"

"I don't know! And I wish you'd stop wondering about things that can't make any difference to us. I'm going back," Taran said. "I don't know how I'm going to climb onto that shelf, but I can certainly do it a lot more easily than digging through a wall."

"Well," said Eilonwy, "it is very strange and all. I'm sure I don't know where we are."

"I knew we'd end up being lost. I could have told you that."

"I didn't say I was lost," the girl protested. "I only said I didn't know where I was. There's a big difference. When you're lost, you really don't know where you are. When you just don't happen to know where you are at the moment, that's something else. I know I'm underneath Spiral Castle, and that's quite good for a start."

"You're splitting hairs," Taran said. "Lost is lost. You're worse than Dallben."

"Who is Dallben?"

"Dallben is my — oh, never mind!" His face grim, Taran began retracing his steps.

Eilonwy hurried to join him. "We could have a look into one of the side passageways," she called.

Taran disregarded the suggestion. Nevertheless, approaching the next branching gallery, he slowed his steps and peered briefly into the gloom.

"Go ahead," Eilonwy urged. "Let's try this one. It seems as good as any."

"Hush!" Taran bent his head and listened intently. From a distance came a faint whispering and rustling. "There's something..."

"Well, by all means let's find out what," said Eilonwy, prodding Taran in the back. "Go ahead, will you?"

Taran took a few cautious steps. The passage here was lower and seemed to slope still farther down. With Eilonwy beside him, he continued gingerly, setting each foot carefully, remembering the sudden, sickening fall that had brought him there in the first place. The whispering became a high keening, a wail of torment. It was as though voices had been spun out like threads, twisted taut, ready to snap. An icy current wove through the air, carrying along with it hollow sighs and a swell of dull mutterings. There were other sounds, too; raspings and shriekings, like sword points dragged over stones. Taran felt his hands tremble; he hesitated a moment and gestured for Eilonwy to stay behind him.

"Give me the light," he whispered, "and wait for me here."

"Do you think it's ghosts?" Eilonwy asked. "I don't have any beans to spit at them, and that's about the only thing that will really do for a ghost. But you know I don't think it's ghosts at all. I've never heard one, though I suppose they could sound like that if they wanted to, but I don't see why they should bother. No, I think it's wind making all those noises."

"Wind? How could there be... Wait," Taran said. "You may be right, at that. There might be an opening." Closing his ears to the horrifying sounds and preferring to think of them as draughts of air rather than spectral voices, Taran quickened his pace. Eilonwy, paying no attention to his order to wait, strode along with him.

They soon arrived at the end of the passage. Once more, fallen stones blocked their way, but this time there was a narrow, jagged gap. From it, the wailing grew louder, and Taran felt a cold ribbon of air on his face. He thrust the light into the opening, but even the golden rays could not pierce the curtain of shadows. Taran slid cautiously past the barrier; Eilonwy followed.

They entered a low-ceilinged chamber, and as they did, the light flickered under the weight of the darkness. At first, Taran could make out only indistinct shapes, touched with a feeble green glow. The voices screamed in trembling rage. Despite the chill wind, Taran's forehead was clammy. He raised the light and took another step forwards. The shapes grew clearer. Now he distinguished outlines of shields hanging from the walls and piles of swords and spears. His foot struck something. He bent to look and sprang back again, stifling a cry. It was the withered corpse of a man — a warrior fully armed. Another lay beside him, and another, in a circle of ancient dead guarding a high stone slab on which a shadowy figure lay at full length.

Eilonwy paid scant attention to the warriors, having found something more interesting to her. "I'm sure Achren hasn't any idea all this is here," she whispered, pointing to heaps of otter-skin robes and great earthen jars overflowing with jewels. Weapons glistened amid stacks of helmets; woven baskets held brooches, collar-pieces, and chains.

"She'd have hauled it out long ago; she loves jewellery, you know, though it doesn't become her one bit."

"Surely it is the barrow of the king who built this castle," Taran said in a hushed voice. He stepped past the warriors and drew near the figure on the slab. Rich raiment clothed the body; polished stones glowed in his broad belt. The clawed hands still grasped the jewelled hilt of a sword, as if ready to unsheathe it. Taran recoiled in fear and horror. The skull seemed to grimace in defiance, daring a stranger to despoil the royal treasures.

As Taran turned, a gust of wind caught his face. "I think there is a passage," he called, "there, in the far wall." He ran in the direction of the ghostly cries.

Close to the ground, a tunnel opened; he could smell fresh air, and his lungs drank deeply. "Hurry," he urged.

Taran snatched a sword from a warrior's bony hand and scrambled into the tunnel.

The tunnel was the narrowest they had encountered. Flat on his belly, Taran squeezed and fought his way over the loose stones. Behind him, he heard Eilonwy gasping and struggling. Then a new sound began, a distant booming and throbbing. The earth shuddered as the pounding increased. Suddenly the passageway convulsed, the hidden roots of trees sprang up, the ground split beneath Taran, heaving and crumbling. In another instant, he was flung out at the bottom of a rocky slope.

A great crash resounded deep within the hill. Spiral Castle, high above him, was bathed in blue fire. A sudden gale nearly battered Taran to the ground. A tree of lightning crackled in the sky. Behind him, Eilonwy called for help.

She was half in, half out of the narrow passage. As Taran wrestled with the fallen stones, the walls of Spiral

Castle shook like grey rags. The towers lurched madly. Taran clawed away clumps of earth and roots.

"I'm all tangled up with the sword," Eilonwy panted. "The scabbard's caught on something."

Taran heaved at the last rock. "What sword?" he said through gritted teeth. He seized Eilonwy under the arms and pulled her free.

"Oof!" she gasped. "I feel as if I had all my bones taken apart and put together wrong. The sword? You said you needed weapons, didn't you? And you took one, so I thought I might as well, too."

In a violent explosion that seemed ripped from the very centre of the earth, Spiral Castle crumbled in on itself. The mighty stones of its walls split like twigs, their jagged ends thrusting at the sky. Then a deep silence fell. The wind was still; the air oppressive.

"Thank you for saving my life," said Eilonwy. "For an Assistant Pig-Keeper, I must say you are quite courageous. It's wonderful when people surprise you that way.

"I wonder what happened to Achren," she went on. "She'll really be furious," she added with a delighted laugh, "and probably blame everything on me, for she's always punishing me for things I haven't even thought of yet."

"If Achren is under those stones, she'll never punish anyone again," Taran said. "But I don't think we'd better stay to find out." He buckled on his sword.

The blade Eilonwy had taken from the barrow was too long for the girl to wear comfortably at her waist, so she had slung it from her shoulder.

Taran looked at the weapon with surprise. "Why – that's the sword the king was holding."

"Naturally," said Eilonwy. "It should be the best one, shouldn't it?" She picked up the glowing sphere. "We're at the far side of the castle, what used to be the castle. Your friend is down there, among those trees – assuming he waited for you. I'd be surprised if he did, with all this going on..."

They ran towards the grove. Ahead, Taran saw the shadowy forms of a cloaked figure and a white horse. "There they are!" he cried.

"Gwydion!" he called. "Gwydion!"

The moon swung from behind the clouds. The figure turned. Taran stopped short in the sudden brightness and his jaw dropped. He had never seen this man before.

CHAPTER NINE

Fflewddur Fflam

Taran's sword leaped out. The man in the cloak hurriedly dropped Melyngar's bridle and darted behind a tree. Taran swung the blade. Pieces of bark sprayed the air. While the stranger ducked back and forth, Taran slashed and thrust, hacking wildly at bushes and branches.

"You're not Gwydion!" he shouted.

"Never claimed I was," the stranger shouted back. "If you think I'm Gwydion, you're dreadfully mistaken."

"Come out of there," Taran ordered, thrusting again.

"Certainly not while you're swinging that enormous — here now, watch that! Great Belin, I was safer in Achren's dungeon!"

"Come out now or you won't be able to," Taran shouted. He redoubled his attack, ripping furiously through the underbrush.

"Truce! Truce!" called the stranger. "You can't smite an unarmed man!"

Eilonwy, who had been a few paces behind Taran, ran up and seized his arm. "Stop it!" she cried. "That's no way to treat your friend, after I went to all the bother of rescuing him."

Taran shook off Eilonwy. "What treachery is this!" he shouted. "You left my companion to die! You've been with Achren all along. I should have known it. You're no better than she is!" With a cry of anguish, he raised his sword.

Eilonwy ran sobbing into the woods. Taran dropped the blade and stood with bowed head.

The stranger ventured from behind the tree. "Truce?" he inquired again. "Believe me, if I'd known it was going to cause all this trouble I wouldn't have listened to that redheaded girl."

Taran did not raise his head.

The stranger took a few more cautious steps. "Humblest apologies for disappointing you," he said. "I'm awfully flattered you mistook me for Prince Gwydion.

There's hardly any resemblance, except possibly a certain air of..."

"I do not know who you are," Taran said bitterly. "I do know that a brave man has bought your life for you."

"I am Fflewddur Fflam Son of Godo," the stranger said, bowing deeply, "a bard of the harp at your service."

"I have no need of bards," Taran said. "A harp will not bring my companion to life."

"Lord Gwydion is dead?" Fflewddur Fflam asked. "Those are sorrowful tidings. He is a kinsman and I owe allegiance to the House of Don. But why do you blame his death on me? If Gwydion has bought my life, at least tell me how, and I shall mourn with you."

"Go your way," said Taran. "It is no fault of yours. I trusted Gwydion's life to a traitor and liar. My own life should be forfeit."

"Those are hard words to apply to a winsome lass," said the bard. "Especially one who isn't here to defend herself."

"I want no explanation from her," he said. "There is nothing she can tell me. She can lose herself in the forest, for all I care."

"If she's as much of a traitor and a liar as you say," Fflewddur remarked, "then you're letting her off easily. You may not want her explanation, but I'm quite sure Gwydion would. Allow me to suggest you go and find her before she strays too far."

Taran nodded. "Yes," he said coldly, "Gwydion shall have justice."

He turned on his heel and walked towards the trees. Eilonwy had gone no great distance; he could see the glow of the sphere a few paces ahead, where the girl sat on a boulder in a clearing. She looked small and thin; her head was pressed into her hands, and her shoulders shook.

"Now you've made me cry!" she burst out, as Taran approached. "I hate crying; it makes my nose feel like a melted icicle. You've hurt my feelings, you stupid Assistant Pig-Keeper, and all for something that's your own fault to begin with."

Taran was so taken aback that he began to stammer.

"Yes," cried Eilonwy, "it's every bit your fault! You were so close-mouthed about the man you wanted me to rescue, and you kept talking about your friend in the other cell. Very well, I rescued whoever it was in the other cell."

"You didn't tell me there was anyone else in the dungeon."

"There wasn't," Eilonwy insisted. "Fflewddur Fflam or whatever he calls himself was the only one."

"Then where is my companion?" Taran demanded. "Where is Gwydion?"

"I don't know," Eilonwy said. "He wasn't in Achren's dungeon, that's sure. What's more, he never was."

Taran realized the girl was speaking the truth. As his memory returned, he recalled that Gwydion had been with him only briefly; he had not seen the guards put him in a cell; Taran had only guessed at that.

"What could she have done with him?"

"I haven't any idea in the world," Eilonwy said and sniffed. "She could have brought him to her chambers, or locked him in the tower – there's a dozen places she could have hidden him. All you needed to say was, 'Go and rescue a man named Gwydion,' and I would have found him. But no, you had to be so clever about it and keep everything to yourself..."

Taran's heart sank. "I must go back to the castle and find him. Will you show me where Achren might have imprisoned him?"

"There's nothing left of the castle," said Eilonwy. "Besides, I'm not sure I'm going to help you any more at all, after the way you've behaved; and calling me those horrid names, that's like putting caterpillars in somebody's hair." She tossed her head, put her chin in the air, and refused to look at him.

"I accused you falsely," Taran said. "My shame is as deep as my sorrow."

Eilonwy, without lowering her chin, gave him a sidelong glance. "I should think it would be."

"I shall seek him alone," said Taran. "You are right in

refusing to help. It is no concern of yours." He turned and started out of the clearing.

"Well, you don't have to agree with me so quickly," Eilonwy cried. She slid off the boulder and hastened after him.

Fflewddur Fflam was still waiting when they returned. In the light of Eilonwy's sphere, Taran had a better view of this unexpected arrival. The bard was tall and lanky, with a long, pointed nose. His great shock of bright yellow hair burst out in all directions, like a ragged sun. His jacket and leggings were patched at knees and elbows, and sewn with large, clumsy stitches – the work, Taran was certain, of the bard himself. A harp with a beautiful, sweeping curve was slung from his shoulder, but otherwise he looked nothing at all like the bards Taran had learned about from *The Book of Three*.

"So it seems that I've been rescued by mistake," Fflewddur said, after Taran explained what had happened. "I should have known it would turn out to be something like that. I kept asking myself, crawling along those beastly tunnels, who could possibly be interested whether I was languishing in a dungeon or not?"

"I am going back to the castle," Taran said. "There may be hope that Gwydion still lives."

"By all means," cried the bard, his eyes lighting up. "A Fflam to the rescue! Storm the castle! Carry it by assault! Batter down the gates!"

"There's not much of it left to storm," said Eilonwy.

"Oh?" said Fflewddur, with disappointment. "Very well, we shall do the best we can."

At the summit of the hill, the mighty blocks of stone lay as if crushed by a giant fist. Only the square arch of the gate remained upright, gaunt as a bone. In the moonlight, the ruins seemed already ancient. Shreds of mist hung over the shattered tower. Achren had learned of his escape, Taran guessed, for at the moment of the castle's destruction, she had sent out a company of guards. Amid the rubble, their bodies sprawled motionless as the stones.

With growing despair, Taran climbed over the ruins. The foundations of the castle had collapsed. The walls had fallen inwards. The bard and Eilonwy helped Taran try to shift one or two of the broken rocks, but the work was beyond their strength.

At last, the exhausted Taran shook his head. "We can do no more," he murmured. "This shall stand as Gwydion's burial mound." He stood a moment, looking silently over the desolation, then turned away.

Fflewddur suggested taking weapons from the bodies of the guards. He equipped himself with a dagger, sword, and spear; in addition to the blade she had taken from the barrow, Eilonwy carried a slim dagger at her waist. Taran collected as many bows and quivers of arrows as he could carry. The group was now lightly but effectively armed.

With heavy hearts, the little band made their way down the slope. Melyngar followed docilely, her head bowed, as if she understood that she would not see her master again.

"I must leave this evil place," Taran cried. "I am impatient to be gone from here. Spiral Castle has brought me only grief; I have no wish to see it again."

"What has it brought the rest of us?" Eilonwy asked. "You make it sound as though we were just sitting around having a splendid time while you moan and take on."

Taran stopped abruptly. "I – I'm sorry," he said. "I didn't mean it that way."

"Furthermore," said Eilonwy, "you're mistaken if you think I'm going to go marching through the woods in the middle of the night."

"And I," put in Fflewddur, "I don't mind telling you I'm so tired I could sleep on Achren's doorstep."

"We all need rest," Taran said. "But I don't trust Achren, alive or dead, and we still know nothing of the Cauldron-Born. If they escaped, they may be looking for us right now. No matter how tired we are, it would be foolhardy to stay this close."

Eilonwy and Fflewddur agreed to continue on for a little distance. After a time, they found a spot well protected by trees, and flung themselves wearily to the turf. Taran unsaddled Melyngar, thankful the girl had thought to bring along Gwydion's gear. He found a cloak in a saddlebag and handed it to Eilonwy. The bard wrapped himself in his own tattered garment and set his harp carefully on a gnarled root.

Taran stood the first watch. Thoughts of the livid warriors still haunted him, and he saw their faces in every shadow. As the night wore on, the passage of a forest creature or the restless sighing of wind in the leaves made him start. The bushes rustled. This time it was not the wind. He heard a faint scratching, and his hand flew to his sword.

A figure bounded into the moonlight and rolled up to Taran.

"Crunchings and munchings?" whimpered a voice.

"Who is your peculiar friend?" asked the bard, sitting up and looking curiously at this new arrival.

"For an Assistant Pig-Keeper," remarked Eilonwy, "you do keep strange company. Where did you find it? And what is it? I've never seen anything like that in my life."

"He is no friend of mine," cried Taran. "He is a miserable, sneaking wretch who deserted us as soon as we were attacked."

"No, no!" Gurgi protested, whimpering and bobbing his matted head. "Poor humble Gurgi is always faithful to mighty lords — what joy to serve them, even with shakings and breakings."

"Tell the truth," said Taran. "You ran off when we needed you most."

"Slashings and gashings are for noble lords, not for poor, weak Gurgi. Oh, fearsome whistlings of blades! Gurgi ran to look for help, mighty lord."

"You didn't succeed in finding any," Taran said angrily.

"Oh, sadness!" Gurgi moaned. "There was no help for brave warriors. Gurgi went far, far, with great squeakings and shriekings."

"I'm sure you did," Taran said.

"What else can unhappy Gurgi do? He is sorry to see great warriors in distress, oh, tears of misery! But in battle, what would there be for poor Gurgi except hurtful guttings and cuttings of his throat?"

"It wasn't very brave," said Eilonwy, "but it wasn't altogether stupid, either. I don't see what advantage there was for him to be chopped up, especially if he wasn't any help to you in the first place."

"Oh, wisdom of a noble lady!" Gurgi cried, throwing himself at Eilonwy's feet. "If Gurgi had not gone seeking help, he would not be here to serve you now. But he is here! Yes, yes, faithful Gurgi returns to beatings and bruisings from the terrifying warrior!"

"Just keep out of my sight," Taran said, "or you really will have something to complain about."

Gurgi snuffled. "Gurgi hastens to obey, mighty lord.

He will say no more, not even whisperings of what he saw. No, he will not disturb the sleepings of powerful heroes. See how he leaves, with tearful farewells."

"Come back here immediately," Taran called.

Gurgi brightened. "Crunchings?"

"Listen to me," Taran said, "there's hardly enough to go round, but I'll give you a fair share of what we have. After that, you'll have to find your own munchings."

Gurgi nodded. "Many more hosts march in the valley with sharp spears – oh, many more. Gurgi watches so quietly and cleverly, he does not ask them for help. No, they would only give harmful hurtings."

"What's this, what's this?" cried Fflewddur. "A great host? I should love to see them. I always enjoy processions and that sort of thing."

"The enemies of the House of Don are gathering," Taran hurriedly told the bard. "Gwydion and I saw them before we were captured. Now, if Gurgi speaks the truth, they have gathered reinforcements."

The bard sprang to his feet. "A Fflam never shrinks from danger! The mightier the foe, the greater the glory! We shall seek them out, set upon them! The bards shall sing our praises for ever!"

Carried away by Fflewddur's enthusiasm, Taran seized his sword. Then he shook his head, remembering Gwydion's words in the forest near Caer Dallben. "No – no," he said slowly, "it would be folly to think of attacking them." He smiled quickly at Fflewddur. "The bards would sing of us," he admitted, "but we'd be in no position to appreciate it."

Fflewddur sat down again, disappointed.

"You can talk about the bards singing your praises all you want," said Eilonwy. "I'm in no mood to do battle. I'm going to sleep." With that, she curled up on the ground and pulled the cloak over her head.

Still unconvinced, Fflewddur settled himself against a tree root for his turn at guard. Gurgi curled up at Eilonwy's feet. Exhausted though he was, Taran lay awake. In his mind, he saw again the Horned King and heard the screams from the flaming cages.

He sat up quickly. Grieving for his companion, he had forgotten what had brought him here. His own quest had been for Hen Wen; Gwydion's, to warn the Sons of Don. Taran's head spun. With his companion surely dead, should he now try to make his way to Caer Dathyl? What, then, would become of Hen Wen? Everything had ceased to be simple. He yearned for the peacefulness of Caer Dallben, yearned even to weed the vegetable gardens and make horseshoes. He turned restlessly, finding no answer. At last, his weariness overcame him and he slept, plunged in nightmares.

CHAPTER TEN

The Sword Dyrnwyn

It was full daylight when Taran opened his eyes. Gurgi was already sniffing hungrily at the saddlebags. Taran rose quickly and shared out as much of the remaining provisions as he dared, keeping a small amount in reserve, since he had no idea how difficult it would be to find food during the coming journey. In the course of the restless night, he had reached his decision, though at present he refrained from speaking of it, still unsure he had chosen wisely. For the moment he concentrated on a meagre breakfast.

Gurgi, sitting cross-legged, devoured his food with so many outcries of pleasure and loud smackings of his lips that he seemed to be eating twice as much as he really did. Fflewddur bolted his scant portion as though he had not enjoyed a meal for at least five days. Eilonwy was more interested in the sword she had taken from the barrow. It lay across her knees and, with a perplexed frown, the tip of her tongue between her lips, the girl was studying the weapon curiously.

As Taran grew near, Eilonwy snatched the sword away. "Well," said Taran, with a laugh, "you needn't act as if I were going to steal it from you." Although jewels studded the hilt and pommel, the scabbard was battered, discoloured, nearly black with age. For all that, it had an air of ancient lineage, and Taran was eager to hold it. "Come," he said, "let me see the blade."

"I dare not," cried Eilonwy, to Taran's great surprise. He saw that her face was solemn and almost fearful.

"There is a symbol of power on the scabbard," Eilonwy continued. "I've seen this mark before, on some of Achren's things. It always means something forbidden. Of course, all Achren's things are like that, but some are more forbidden than others.

"There's another inscription, too," said Eilonwy, frowning again. "But it's in the Old Writing." She stamped her foot. "Oh, I do wish Achren had finished teaching it to me. I can almost make it out, but not quite, and there's nothing more irritating. It's like not finishing what you started out to say."

Fflewddur came up just then and he, too, peered at the strange weapon. "Comes from a barrow, eh?" The bard shook his spiky, yellow head and whistled. "I suggest getting rid of it immediately. Never had much confidence in things you find in barrows. It's a bad business having anything to do with them. You can't be sure where else they've been and who's had them."

"If it's an enchanted weapon," Taran began, more interested than ever in getting his hands on the sword, "shouldn't we keep it..."

"Oh, do be quiet," Eilonwy cried. "I can't hear myself think. I don't see what you're both talking about, getting rid of it or not getting rid of it. After all, it's mine, isn't it? I found it and carried it out, and almost got stuck in a dirty old tunnel because of it."

"Bards are supposed to understand these things," Taran said.

"Naturally," Fflewddur answered, smiling confidently and putting his long nose closer to the scabbard. "These inscriptions are all pretty much the same. I see this one's on the scabbard rather than the blade. It says, oh, something like 'Beware My Wrath' — the usual sentiments."

At that moment there was a loud twang. Fflewddur

blinked. One of his harp strings had snapped. "Excuse me," he said, and went to see about his instrument.

"It doesn't say anything at all like that," Eilonwy declared. "I can read some of it now. Here, it starts near the hilt and goes winding around like ivy. I was looking at it the wrong way. It says *Dyrnwyn*, first. I don't know whether that's the name of the sword or the name of the king. Oh, yes, that's the name of the sword; here it is again:

DRAW DYRNWYN, ONLY THOU
OF ROYAL BLOOD,
TO RULE, TO STRIKE THE...

"Something or other," Eilonwy went on. "It's very faint; I can't see it. The letters are worn too smooth. No, that's odd. They aren't worn; they've been scratched out. They must have been cut deeply, because there's still a trace. But I can't read the rest. This word looks as if it might be death..." She shuddered. "That's not very cheerful."

"Let me unsheathe it," Taran urged again. "There might be more on the blade."

"Certainly not," said Eilonwy. "I told you it had a symbol of power and I'm bound by it – that's elementary."

"Achren cannot bind you any longer."

"It isn't Achren," Eilonwy answered. "I only said she had things with the same mark. This is a stronger enchantment than any she could make, I'm quite sure. I wouldn't dare to draw it, and I don't intend letting you, either. Besides, it says *only royal blood* and doesn't mention a word about Assistant Pig-Keepers."

"How can you tell I haven't royal blood?" Taran asked, bristling. "I wasn't *born* an Assistant Pig-Keeper. For all you know, my father might have been a king. It happens all the time in *The Book of Three*."

"I never heard of *The Book of Three*," said Eilonwy. "But in the first place, I don't think it's good enough to be a king's son or even a king himself. Royal blood is just a way of translating; in the Old Writing, it didn't mean only having royal relatives – anybody can have those. It meant – oh, I don't know what you'd call it. Something very special. And it seems to me that if you have it, you don't need to wonder whether you have it."

"So, of course," said Taran, nettled by the girl's remarks, "you've made up your mind that I'm not – whatever it is."

"I didn't mean to offend you," Eilonwy said quickly. "For an Assistant Pig-Keeper, I think you're quite remarkable. I even think you're the nicest person I've ever met in my life. It's just that I'm forbidden to let you have the sword and that's that."

"What will you do with it, then?"

"Keep it, naturally. I'm not going to drop it down a well, am I?"

Taran snorted. "You'll make a fine sight – a little girl carrying a sword."

"I am not a little girl," said Eilonwy, tossing her hair in exasperation. "Among my people in the olden days, the Sword Maidens did battle beside the men."

"It's not the olden days now," Taran said. "Instead of a sword, you should be carrying a doll."

Eilonwy, with a squeal of vexation, raised a hand to slap at Taran, when Fflewddur Fflam returned.

"Here now," said the bard, "no squabbling; there's not a bit of use to it." With a large key he tightened the wooden peg holding the newly repaired harp string.

Eilonwy turned her irritation on Fflewddur. "That inscription was a very important one. It didn't say anything about bewaring anyone's wrath. You didn't read it right at all. You're a fine bard, if you can't make out the writing on an enchanted sword."

"Well, you see, the truth of the matter," said Fflewddur, clearing his throat and speaking with much hesitation, "is this way. I'm not officially a bard."

"I didn't know there were *un*official bards," Eilonwy remarked.

"Oh, yes indeed," said Fflewddur. "At least in my case. I'm also a king."

"A king?" Taran said. "Sire..." He dropped to one knee.

"None of that, none of that," said Fflewddur. "I don't

bother with it any more."

"Where is your kingdom?" Eilonwy asked.

"Several days' journey east of Caer Dathyl," said Fflewddur. "It is a vast realm..."

At this, Taran heard another jangling.

"Drat the thing," said the bard. "There go two more strings. As I was saying. Yes, well, it is actually a rather *small* kingdom in the north, very dull and dreary. So I gave it up. I'd always loved barding and wandering – and that's what I decided to do."

"I thought bards had to study a great deal," Eilonwy said. "A person can't just go and decide..."

"Yes, that was one of the problems," said the former king. "I studied; I did quite well in the examinations..." A small string at the upper end of the harp broke with a high-pitched tinkle and curled up like an ivy tendril. "I did quite *poorly*," he went on, "and the Council of Bards wouldn't admit me. Really, they want you to know so much these days. Volumes and volumes of poetry, and chants and music and calculating the seasons, and history; and all kinds of alphabets you spell out on your fingers, and secret signs – a man couldn't hope to cram it all into his skull.

"The Council were very nice to me," continued Fflewddur. "Taliesin, the Chief Bard himself, presented me with this harp. He said it was exactly what I needed. I sometimes wonder if he was really doing me a favour. It's a very nice harp, but I have such trouble with the strings. I'd throw it away and get another, but it has a beautiful tone; I should never find one as good. If only the beastly strings..."

"They do seem to break frequently," Eilonwy began.

"Yes, that's so," Fflewddur admitted, a little sheepishly. "I've noticed it usually happens when — well, I'm an emotional sort of fellow, and I do get carried away. I might, ah, readjust the facts slightly; purely for dramatic effect, you understand."

"If you'd stop readjusting the facts quite as much," Eilonwy said, "perhaps you wouldn't have that trouble with the harp."

"Yes, I suppose," said the bard with a sigh. "I try, but it's hard, very hard. As a king, you get into the habit. Sometimes I think I pass more time fixing strings than playing. But, there it is. You can't have everything."

"Where were you journeying when Achren captured you?" Taran asked.

"No place in particular," said Fflewddur. "That's one advantage. You don't have to hurry to get somewhere. You keep moving, and next thing you know, there you are. Unfortunately, in this case, it was Achren's dungeon. She didn't care for my playing. That woman has no ear for music," he added, shuddering.

"Sire," Taran said, "I ask a boon."

"Please," said the former king, "Fflewddur will do very well. A boon? Delighted! I haven't done any boon granting since I gave up the throne."

Fflewddur Fflam and Eilonwy seated themselves on the turf, while Taran recounted his search for Hen Wen and what Gwydion had told him of the Horned King and the rising of the cantrevs. Gurgi, having finished his meal, sidled over and squatted on a hillock to listen.

"There is no doubt in my mind," Taran went on, "the Sons of Don must have news of the uprising before the Horned King strikes. If he triumphs, Arawn will have Prydain by the throat. I have seen with my own eyes what that means." He felt ill at ease, speaking as if he himself were a war leader in a council hall, but soon the words began to come easier. Perhaps, he thought, because he was speaking for Gwydion.

"I see your plan," Fflewddur interrupted. "You shall keep on looking for your pig, and you want me to warn the warriors of Don. Splendid! I shall start off immediately. And if the hosts of the Horned King overtake me..." The bard slashed and thrust at the air. "They shall know the valour of a Fflam!"

Taran shook his head. "No, I shall journey to Caer Dathyl myself. I do not question your valour," he said to the bard, "but the danger is too great. I ask no one else to face it in my stead."

"When do you intend to seek your pig?" asked Fflewddur.

"My own quest," said Taran, looking at the bard, "must be given up. If it is possible, after the first task is done, I mean to return to it. Until then, I serve only Gwydion. It was I who cost him his life, and it is justice for me to do what I believe he would have done."

"As I grasp the situation," said the bard, "I think you're taking too much blame on yourself. You had no way of knowing Gwydion wasn't in the dungeon."

"It changes nothing," Taran answered. "I have made my decision."

Fflewddur was about to protest, but the firmness of Taran's words silenced the bard. After a moment, he asked, "What is your boon, then?"

"It is twofold," said Taran. "First, tell me how I may reach Caer Dathyl as quickly as possible. Second, I beg you to conduct this girl safely to her own people."

Before Fflewddur could open his mouth, Eilonwy gave an indignant cry and leaped to her feet. "Conducted? I shall be conducted where I please! I'm not going to be sent back, just so I can be sent somewhere else; and it will be another dreary place, you can be sure. No, I shall go to Caer Dathyl, too!"

"There is risk enough," Taran declared, "without having to worry about a girl."

Eilonwy put her hands on her hips. Her eyes flashed. "I don't like being called '*a* girl' and '*this* girl' as if I didn't have a name at all. It's like having your head put in a sack. If you've made your decision, I've made my own. I don't see how you're going to stop me. If *you*," she hurried on, pointing at the bard, "try to conduct me to my mean, stupid kinsmen — and they're hardly related to me in the first place — that harp will be in pieces around your ears!"

Fflewddur blinked and clutched his harp protectively, while Eilonwy went on.

"And if a certain Assistant Pig-Keeper — I won't even mention *his* name — thinks otherwise, he'll be even more mistaken!"

Everyone started talking at once. "Stop it!" cried Taran at the top of his voice. "Very well," he said, after the others grew quiet. "You," he said to Eilonwy, "could be tied up and set on Melyngar. But," he added, raising his hand before the girl could interrupt, "that will not be done. *Not* because of all the commotion you raised, but because I realize now it is best."

The bard looked surprised.

Taran continued. "There is greater safety in greater numbers. Whatever happens, there will be more chance for one of us to reach Caer Dathyl. I believe we should all stay together."

"And faithful Gurgi, too!" shouted Gurgi. "He will

follow! Too many wicked enemies are smirking and lurking to jab him with pointy spears!"

"If he agrees," Taran said, "Fflewddur shall act as guide. But I warn you," he added, glancing at Gurgi and Eilonwy, "nothing must hinder our task."

"Ordinarily," said Fflewddur, "I prefer to be in charge of this type of expedition myself. But," he went on, as Taran was about to protest, "since you are acting for Lord Gwydion, I accept your authority as I would accept his." He bowed low. "A Fflam is yours to command."

"Forward then!" the bard cried. "And if we must give battle, so be it! Why, I've carved my way through walls of spearmen..."

Six harp strings broke at once, and the others strained so tautly they looked on the verge of snapping. While Taran saddled Melyngar, the bard set ruefully to work repairing his harp.

CHAPTER ELEVEN

Flight Through the Hills

At first, Taran offered to let Eilonwy ride Melyngar, but the girl refused.

"I can walk as well as any of you," she cried, so angrily that Taran made no more of it; he had learned to be wary of the girl's sharp tongue. It was agreed that the white mare would carry the weapons taken from Spiral Castle – except the sword Dyrnwyn, of which Eilonwy had appointed herself guardian.

Scratching in the dirt with his dagger point, Fflewddur

Fflam showed Taran the path he intended to follow. "The hosts of the Horned King will surely stay in the Valley of Ystrad. It's the easiest way for an army on the march. Spiral Castle was here," he added, with an angry jab to mark the spot, "west of the River Ystrad. Now, the shortest road would be straight north over these hills."

"That is the one we must take," said Taran, trying hard to make sense of Fflewddur's crisscrossing lines.

"Wouldn't recommend it, my friend. We should be passing a little too near Annuvin. Arawn's strongholds are close to Spiral Castle; and I suggest we keep clear of them. No, what I believe we should do is this: stay on the high ground of the western bank of Ystrad; we can go quite directly, since we needn't follow the valley itself. That way, we can avoid both Annuvin and the Horned King. The four of us can move faster than heavily armed warriors. We shall come out well ahead of them, not too far from Caer Dathyl. From there, we make a dash for it – and our task is done." Fflewddur straightened up, beaming with satisfaction. "There you have it," he said, wiping the dirt from his dagger. "A brilliant strategy. My own war-leader couldn't have arranged it better."

"Yes," said Taran, his head still muddled with the bard's talk of high ground and western banks, "that sounds very reasonable."

They descended to a broad, sun-swept meadow. The morning had turned bright and warm; dew still clung to bending blades of grass. At the head of the travellers strode Fflewddur, stepping out briskly on his long, spindly shanks. The harp jogged on his back; his shabby cloak was rolled over his shoulder. Eilonwy, hair dishevelled by the breeze, the great black sword slung behind her, followed next, with Gurgi immediately after. So many new leaves and twigs had stuck in Gurgi's hair that he had begun to look like a walking beaver dam; he loped along, swinging his arms, shaking his head from side to side, moaning and muttering.

Holding Melyngar's bridle, Taran marched last in line. Except for the weapons lashed to the horse's saddle, these travellers might have been on a spring ramble. Eilonwy chattered gaily; now and then Fflewddur burst into a snatch of song. Taran alone was uneasy. To him, the bright morning felt deceptively gentle; the golden trees seemed to cover dark shadows. He shuddered even in the warmth. His heart was troubled, too, as he watched his companions. In Caer Dallben, he had dreamed of being a hero. But dreaming, he had come to learn, was easy; and at Caer Dallben no lives depended on his judgment. He longed for Gwydion's strength and guidance. His own strength, he feared, was not equal to his task. He turned once for a last look in the direction of Spiral Castle, Gwydion's burial mound. Over the hill crest, stark against the clouds, rose two figures on horseback.

Taran shouted and gestured for his companions to take cover in the woods. Melyngar galloped forwards. In another moment, they were all crouching in a thicket. The horsemen followed along the crest, too far away for Taran to see their faces clearly; but from their rigid postures he could guess at the livid features and dull eyes of the Cauldron-Born.

"How long have they been behind us?" asked Fflewddur. "Have they seen us?"

Taran looked cautiously through the screen of leaves. He pointed towards the slope. "There is your answer," he said.

From the crest the pale Cauldron warriors had turned their horses towards the meadow and were steadily picking their way down the hill. "Hurry," ordered Taran. "We must outrun them."

The group did not return to the meadow, but struck out across the woods. The appearance of the Cauldron-Born now forced them to abandon the path Fflewddur had chosen, but the bard hoped they might throw the warriors off the track and circle back again to higher ground.

Staying close to one another, they moved at a dog trot, not daring to stop even for water. The forest offered a measure of protection from the sun, but after a time the pace began to tell on them. Only Gurgi did not seem fatigued or uncomfortable. He loped steadily along, and the swarms of midges and stinging insects could not penetrate his matted hair. Eilonwy, who proudly insisted she enjoyed running, clung to Melyngar's stirrup.

Taran could not be sure how close the warriors were; he knew the Cauldron-Born could hardly fail to track them, by sound if nothing else, for they no longer attempted to move silently. Speed was their only hope, and long after nightfall they pressed on.

It had become a blind race into darkness, under a moon drowned in heavy clouds. Invisible branches grasped at them or slashed their faces. Eilonwy stumbled once, and Taran pulled her to her feet. The girl faltered again; her head drooped. Taran unstrapped the weapons on Melyngar's saddle, shared out the burden with Fflewddur and Gurgi, and hoisted the protesting Eilonwy to Melyngar's back. She slumped forwards, her cheek pressed against the horse's golden mane.

All night they struggled through the forest, which grew denser the closer they approached the Ystrad valley. By the time the first hesitating light of day appeared, even Gurgi had begun to stumble with fatigue and could barely put one hairy foot in front of the other. Eilonwy had fallen into a slumber so deep that Taran feared she was ill. Her hair lay bedraggled and damp upon her forehead; her face was pallid. With the bard's help, Taran lifted her from the saddle and propped her against a mossy bank. When he ventured to unbuckle the cumbersome sword, Eilonwy opened one eye, made an irritated face, and pulled the blade away from him — with more determination than he had expected.

"You never understand things the first time," Eilonwy murmured, her grip firm on the weapon. "But I imagine Assistant Pig-Keepers are all alike. I told you before you're not to have it, and now I'll tell you for the second time — or is it the third, or fourth? I must have lost count." So saying, she wrapped her arms around the scabbard and dropped back to sleep.

"We must rest here," Taran said to the bard, "if only a little while."

"At the moment," groaned Fflewddur, who had stretched out full length with his toes and nose pointing straight into the air, "I don't care who catches me. I'd welcome Arawn himself, and ask whether he had any breakfast with him."

"The Cauldron-Born might have lost track of us during the night," Taran said hopefully, but without great conviction. "I wish I knew how far we've left them behind — if we've left them behind at all."

Gurgi brightened a little. "Clever Gurgi will know," he cried, "with seekings and peekings."

In another moment, Gurgi was halfway up a tall pine. He clambered easily to the top and perched there like an enormous crow, scanning the land in the direction they had travelled.

Taran, meanwhile, opened the saddlebags. So little food remained that it was hardly worth dividing. He and Fflewddur agreed to give Eilonwy the last of the provisions.

Gurgi had scented food even at the top of the pine tree, and he came scuttling down, snuffling eagerly at the prospect of his crunchings and munchings.

"Stop thinking about eating for a moment," Taran cried. "What did you see?"

"Two warriors are far, but Gurgi sees them — yes, yes, they are riding full of wickedness and fierceness. But there is time for a small crunching," Gurgi pleaded. "Oh, very small for clever, valiant Gurgi."

"There are no more crunchings," said Taran. "If the Cauldron-Born are still on our heels, you had better worry less about food and more about your own skin."

"But Gurgi will find munchings! Very quickly — oh, yes — he is so wise to get them, to comfort the bellies of great noble lords. But they will forget poor Gurgi, and not even give him snips and snaps for his eating."

After a hurried discussion with Fflewddur, who looked as ravenous as Gurgi, Taran agreed they might take a little time to search for berries and edible roots.

"Quite right," said the bard. "Better eat what we can get now, while the Cauldron-Born give us a chance to do it. I shall help you. I know all about foraging in the woods, do it constantly..." The harp tensed and one string showed signs of giving way. "No," he added quickly, "I had better stay with Eilonwy. The truth is, I can't tell a mushroom from a toadstool. I wish I could; it would make the life of a wandering bard considerably more filling."

With cloaks in which to carry back whatever they might find, Taran and Gurgi set off. At a small stream Taran halted to fill Gwydion's leather water flask. Gurgi, sniffing hungrily, ran ahead and disappeared into a strand of rowans. Near the bank of the stream Taran discovered mushrooms, and gathered them hurriedly. Bent on his own search, he paid little heed to Gurgi, until he suddenly heard anguished yelps from behind the trees. Clutching his precious mushrooms, Taran hastened to see what had happened, and came upon Gurgi lying in the middle of the grove, writhing and whimpering, a honeycomb beside him.

At first, Taran thought Gurgi had got himself stung by bees. Then, he saw the creature was in more serious trouble. While Gurgi had climbed for the honey, a dead branch had snapped under his weight. His twisted leg was pinned to the ground with the heavy wood on top of it. Taran heaved the branch away.

The panting Gurgi shook his head. "Poor Gurgi's leg is broken," he moaned. "There will be no more amblings and ramblings for him now!"

Taran bent and examined the injury. The leg was not broken, though badly torn, and swelling rapidly.

"Now Gurgi's head must be chopped off," the creature moaned. "Do it, great lord, do it quickly. Gurgi will squeeze up his eyes so as not to see hurtful slashings."

Taran looked closely at Gurgi. The creature was in earnest. His eyes pleaded with Taran. "Yes, yes," cried Gurgi. "Now, before silent warriors arrive. Gurgi is better dead at your sword than in their hands. Gurgi cannot walk! All will be killed with fearful smitings and bitings. It is better..."

"No," said Taran. "You won't be left in the woods, and you won't have your head chopped off – by me or anyone else." For a moment Taran almost regretted his words. The poor creature was right, he knew. The injury would slow their pace. And Gurgi, like all of them, would be better off dead than in Arawn's grasp. Still, Taran could not bring himself to draw his sword.

"You and Eilonwy can ride Melyngar," Taran said, lifting Gurgi to his feet and putting one of the creature's hairy arms about his shoulder. "Come on, now. One step at a time..."

Taran was exhausted when they reached Eilonwy and the bard. The girl had recovered noticeably and was chattering even faster than before. While Gurgi lay silently on the grass, Taran divided the honeycomb. The portions were pitifully small.

Fflewddur called Taran aside. "Your hairy friend is going to make things difficult," he said quietly. "If Melyngar carries two riders, I don't know how much longer she can keep up."

"That is true," said Taran. "Yet I see nothing else we can do. Would you abandon him? Would you have cut off his head?"

"Absolutely," cried the bard, "in a flash! A Fflam never hesitates. Fortunes of war and all that. Oh, drat and blast! There goes another string. A thick one, too."

When Taran went back to rearrange the weapons they would now be obliged to bear, he was surprised to find a large oak leaf on the ground before his cloak. On the leaf lay Gurgi's tiny portion of honeycomb.

"For great lord," murmured Gurgi. "Gurgi is not hungry for crunchings and munchings today."

Taran looked at the eager face of Gurgi. For the first time they smiled at one another.

"Your gift is generous," Taran said softly, "but you

travel as one of us and you will need all your strength. Keep your share; it is yours by right; and you have more than earned it."

He put his hand gently on Gurgi's shoulder. The wet wolfhound odour did not seem as objectionable as before.

CHAPTER TWELVE

The Wolves

For a time, during the day, Taran believed they had at last outdistanced the Cauldron-Born. But, late that afternoon, the warriors reappeared from behind a distant fringe of trees. Against the westering sun, the long shadows of the horsemen reached across the hill slope towards the flatlands where the small troop struggled onwards.

"We must stand against them sooner or later," Taran said, wiping his forehead. "Let it be now. There can be no victory over the Cauldron-Born, but with luck, we can hold them off for a little while. If Eilonwy and Gurgi can escape, there is still a chance."

Gurgi, draped over Melyngar's saddle, immediately set up a great outcry. "No, no! Faithful Gurgi stays with mighty lord who spared his poor tender head! Happy, grateful Gurgi will fight, too, with slashings and gashings..."

"We appreciate your sentiments," said Fflewddur, "but with that leg of yours, you're hardly up to slashing or gashing or anything at all."

"I'm not going to run, either," Eilonwy put in. "I'm tired of running and having my face scratched and my robe torn, all on account of those stupid warriors." She jumped lightly from the saddle and snatched a bow and a handful of arrows from Taran's pack.

"Eilonwy! Stop!" Taran cried. "These are deathless men! They cannot be killed!"

Although encumbered by the long sword hanging from her shoulder, Eilonwy ran faster than Taran. By the time he caught up with her, she had climbed a hillock and was stringing the bow. The Cauldron Born galloped across the plain. The sun glinted on their drawn swords.

Taran seized the girl by the waist and tried to pull her away. He received a sharp kick in the shins.

"Must you always interfere with everything?" Eilonwy asked indignantly.

Before Taran could reach for her again, she held an

arrow towards the sun and murmured a strange phrase. She nocked the arrow and loosed it in the direction of the Cauldron-Born. The shaft arched upwards and almost disappeared against the bright rays.

Open-mouthed, Taran watched while the shaft began its descent: as the arrow plummeted to earth, long, silvery streamers sprang from its feathers. In an instant, a huge spiderweb glittered in the air and drifted slowly towards the horsemen.

Fflewddur, who had run up just then, stopped in amazement. "Great Belin!" he exclaimed. "What's that? It looks like decorations for a feast!"

The web slowly settled over the Cauldron-Born, but the pallid warriors paid no heed. They spurred their mounts onwards; the strands of the web broke and melted away.

Eilonwy clapped a hand to her mouth. "It didn't work!" she cried, almost in tears. "The way Achren does it, she makes it into a big sticky rope. Oh, it's all gone wrong. I tried to listen behind the door when she was practising, but I've missed something important." She stamped her foot and turned away.

"Take her from here!" Taran called to the bard. He unsheathed his sword and faced the Cauldron-Born. Within moments they would be upon him. But, even as he braced for their onslaught, he saw the horsemen falter. The Cauldron-Born reined up suddenly; then, without a gesture, turned their horses and rode silently back towards the hills.

"It worked! It worked after all!" cried the astonished Fflewddur.

Eilonwy shook her head. "No," she said with discouragement, "something turned them away, but I'm afraid it wasn't my spell." She unstrung the bow and picked up the arrows she had dropped.

"I think I know what it was," Taran said. "They are returning to Arawn. Gwydion told me they could not stay long from Annuvin. Their power must have been waning ever since we left Spiral Castle, and they reached the limit of their strength right here."

"I hope they don't have enough to get back to Annuvin," Eilonwy said. "I hope they fall into pieces or shrivel up like bats."

"I doubt that they will," Taran said, watching the horsemen slowly disappear over the ridge. "They must know how long they can stay and how far they can go, and still return to their master." He gave Eilonwy an admiring glance. "It doesn't matter. They're gone. And that was one of the most amazing things I've ever seen. Gwydion had a mesh of grass that burst into flame; but I've never met anyone else who could make a web like that."

Eilonwy looked at him in surprise. Her cheeks blushed brighter than the sunset. "Why, Taran of Caer Dallben," she said, "I think that's the first polite thing you've said to me."

Then, suddenly, Eilonwy tossed her head and sniffed. "Of course, I should have known; it was the spiderweb. You were more interested in that; you didn't care whether *I* was in danger." She strode haughtily back to Gurgi and Melyngar.

"But that's not true," Taran called. "I – I was..." By then, Eilonwy was out of earshot. Crestfallen, Taran followed her. "I can't make sense out of that girl," he said to the bard. "Can you?"

"Never mind," Fflewddur said. "We aren't really expected to."

That night, they continued to take turns at standing guard, though much of their fear had lifted since the Cauldron‚ Born had vanished. Taran's was the last watch before dawn, and he was awake well before Eilonwy's had ended.

"You had better sleep," Taran told her. "I'll finish the watch for you."

"I'm perfectly able to do my share," said Eilonwy, who had not stopped being irritated at him since the afternoon.

Taran knew better than to insist. He picked up his bow and quiver arrows, stood near the dark trunk of an oak, and looked out across the moon‚silvered meadow. Nearby, Fflewddur snored heartily. Gurgi, whose leg had shown no improvement, stirred restlessly and whimpered in his sleep.

"You know," Taran began, with embarrassed hesitation, "that spiderweb..."

"I don't want to hear any more about it," retorted Eilonwy.

"No — what I meant was: I really was worried about you. But the web surprised me so much I forgot to mention it. It was courageous of you to stand up against the Cauldron warriors. I just wanted to tell you that."

"You took long enough getting around to it," said Eilonwy, a tone of satisfaction in her voice. "But I imagine Assistant Pig-Keepers tend to be slower than what you might expect. It probably comes from the kind of work they do. Don't misunderstand, I think it's awfully important. Only it's the sort of thing you don't often need to be quick about."

"At first," Taran went on, "I thought I would be able to reach Caer Dathyl by myself. I see now that I wouldn't have got even this far without help. It is a good destiny that brings me such brave companions."

"There, you've done it again," Eilonwy cried, so heatedly that Fflewddur choked on one of his snores. "That's all you care about! Someone to help you carry spears and swords and what-all. It could be *anybody* and you'd be just as pleased. Taran of Caer Dallben, I'm not speaking to you any more."

"At home," Taran said — to himself, Eilonwy had already pulled a cloak over her head and was feigning sleep — "nothing ever happened. Now, everything happens. But somehow I can never seem to make it come out right." With a sigh, he held his bow ready and began his turn at guard. Daylight was long in coming.

In the morning, Taran saw that Gurgi's leg was much worse, and he left the campsite to search the woods for healing plants, glad that Coll had taught him the properties of herbs. He made a poultice and set it on Gurgi's wound.

Fflewddur, meanwhile, had begun drawing new maps with his dagger. The Cauldron warriors, explained the bard, had forced the companions too deeply into the Ystrad valley. Returning to their original path would cost them at least two days of hard travel. "Since we're this far," Fflewddur went on, "we might just as well cross Ystrad and follow along the hills, staying out of sight of the Horned King. We'll be only a few days from Caer Dathyl, and if we keep a good pace, we should reach it just in time."

Taran agreed to the new plan. It would, he realized, be more difficult; but he judged Melyngar could still carry the unfortunate Gurgi, as long as the companions shared the burden of the weapons. Eilonwy, having forgotten she was not speaking to Taran, again insisted on walking.

A day's march brought them to the banks of the Ystrad.

Taran stole cautiously ahead. Looking down the broad

valley, he saw a moving dust cloud. When he hurried back and reported this to Fflewddur, the bard clapped him on the shoulder.

"We're ahead of them," he said. "That is excellent news. I was afraid they'd be much closer to us and we'd have to wait for nightfall to cross Ystrad. We've saved half a day! Hurry now and we'll be into the foothills of Eagle Mountains before sundown!"

With his precious harp held above his head, Fflewddur plunged into the river, and the others followed. Here, the Ystrad ran shallow, scarcely above Eilonwy's waist, and the companions forded it with little difficulty. Nevertheless, they emerged cold and dripping, and the setting sun neither dried nor warmed them.

Leaving the Ystrad behind, the companions climbed slopes steeper and rockier than any they had travelled before. Perhaps it was only his imagination, but the air of the land around Spiral Castle had seemed, to Taran, heavy and oppressive. Approaching the Eagle Mountains, Taran felt his burden lighten, as he inhaled the dry, spicy scent of pine.

He had planned to continue the march throughout most of the night; but Gurgi's condition had worsened, obliging Taran to call a halt. Despite the herbs, Gurgi's leg was badly inflamed, and he shivered with fever. He looked thin and sad; the suggestion of crunchings and munchings could not rouse him. Even Melyngar showed concern. As Gurgi lay with his eyes half-closed, his parched lips tight against his teeth, the white mare nuzzled him delicately, whinnying and blowing out her breath anxiously, as if attempting to comfort him as best she could.

Taran risked lighting a small fire. He and Fflewddur stretched Gurgi out beside it. While Eilonwy held up the suffering creature's head and gave him a drink from the leather flask, Taran and the bard moved a little away and spoke quietly between themselves.

"I have done all I know," Taran said. "If there is anything else, it lies beyond my skill." He shook his head sorrowfully. "He has failed badly today, and there is so little of him left I believe I could pick him up with one hand."

"Caer Dathyl is not far away," said Fflewddur, "but our friend, I fear, may not live to see it."

That night, wolves howled in the darkness beyond the fire.

All next day, the wolves followed them; sometimes silently, sometimes barking as if in signal to one another. They remained always out of bow shot, but Taran caught sight of the lean, grey shapes flickering in and out of the scrubby trees.

"As long as they don't come any closer," he said to the bard, "we needn't worry about them."

"Oh, they won't attack us," Fflewddur answered. "Not now, at any rate. They can be infuriatingly patient if they know someone's wounded." He turned an anxious glance towards Gurgi. "For them, it's just a matter of waiting."

"Well, I must say you're a cheerful one," remarked Eilonwy. "You sound as if all we had to look forward to was being gobbled up."

"If they attack, we shall stand them off," Taran said quietly. "Gurgi was willing to give up his life for us; I can do no less for him. Above all, we must not lose heart so close to the end of our journey."

"A Fflam never loses heart!" cried the bard. "Come wolves or what have you!"

Nevertheless, uneasiness settled over the companions as the grey shapes continued trailing them; and Melyngar, docile and obedient until now, turned skittish. The golden-maned horse tossed her head and rolled her eyes at every attempt to lead her.

To make matters worse, Fflewddur declared their progress through the hills was too slow.

"If we go any farther east," said the bard, "we'll run into some really high mountains. The condition we're in, we couldn't possibly climb them. But here, we're practically walled in. Every path has led us roundabout. The cliffs there," he went on, pointing towards the towering mass of rock to his left, "are too rugged to get over. I had thought we'd find a pass before now. Well, that's the way of it. We can only keep on bearing north as much as possible."

"The wolves didn't seem to have any trouble finding their way," said Eilonwy.

"My dear girl," answered the bard, with some indignation, "if I were able to run on four legs and sniff my dinner a mile away, I doubt I'd have any difficulties either."

Eilonwy giggled. "I'd love to see you try," she said.

"We do have someone who can run on four legs," Taran said suddenly. "Melyngar! If anyone can find their way to Caer Dathyl, she can."

The bard snapped his fingers. "That's it!" he cried. "Every horse knows its way home! It's worth trying – and we can't be worse off than we are now."

"For an Assistant Pig-Keeper," said Eilonwy to Taran, "you do come up with some interesting ideas now and then."

When the companions started off again, Taran dropped the bridle and gave Melyngar her head. With the half-conscious Gurgi bound to her saddle, the white horse trotted swiftly ahead at a determined gait.

By mid-afternoon, Melyngar discovered one pass which, Fflewddur admitted, he himself would have overlooked. As the day wore on, Melyngar led them swiftly through rocky defiles to high ridges. It was all the companions could do to keep up with her. When she cantered into a long ravine, Taran lost sight of her for a moment and hurried forwards in time to glimpse the mare as she turned sharply around an outcropping of white stone.

Calling the bard and Eilonwy to follow quickly, Taran ran ahead. He stopped suddenly. To his left, on a high shelf of rock, crouched an enormous wolf with golden eyes and lolling red tongue. Before Taran could draw his sword, the lean animal sprang.

CHAPTER THIRTEEN

The Hidden Valley

The impact of the heavy, furry body caught Taran full in the chest, and sent him tumbling. As he fell, he caught a glimpse of Fflewddur. The bard, too, had been borne to earth under the paws of another wolf. Eilonwy still stood, though a third animal crouched in front of her.

Taran's hand flew to his sword. The grey wolf seized his arm. The animal's teeth, however, did not sink into his flesh, but held him in an unshakeable grip.

At the end of the ravine a huge, robed figure suddenly

appeared. Melyngar stood behind him. The man raised his arm and spoke a command. Immediately, the wolf holding Taran relaxed his jaws and drew away, as obediently as a dog. The man strode towards Taran, who scrambled to his feet.

"You saved our lives," Taran began. "We are grateful."

The man spoke again to the wolves and the animals crowded around him, whining and wagging their tails. He was a strange-looking figure, broad and muscular, with the vigour of an ancient but sturdy tree. His white hair reached below his shoulders and his beard hung to his waist. Around his forehead he wore a narrow band of gold, set with a single blue jewel.

"From these creatures," he said, in a deep voice that was stern but not unkind, "your lives were never in danger. But you must leave this place. It is not an abode for the race of men."

"We were lost," Taran said. "We had been following our horse..."

"Melyngar?" The man turned a pair of keen grey eyes on Taran. Under his deep brow they sparkled like frost in a valley. "Melyngar brought me four of you? I understood young Gurgi was alone. By all means, then, if you are friends of Melyngar. It is Melyngar, isn't it? She looks so much like her mother; and there are so many I cannot always keep track of the names."

"I know who you are," cried Taran. "You are Medwyn!"

"Am I now?" the man answered with a smile that furrowed his face. "Yes, I have been called Medwyn. But how should you know that?"

"I am Taran of Caer Dallben. Gwydion Prince of Don was my companion, and he spoke of you before – before his death. He was journeying to Caer Dathyl, as we are now. I never hoped to find you."

"You were quite right," Medwyn answered. "You could not have found me. Only the animals know my valley. Melyngar led you here. Taran, you say? Of Caer Dallben?" He put an enormous hand to his forehead. "Let me see. Yes, there are visitors from Caer Dallben, I am sure."

Taran's heart leaped. "Hen Wen!" he cried.

Medwyn gave him a puzzled glance. "Were you seeking her? Now, that is curious. No, she is not here."

"But I had thought..."

"We will speak of Hen Wen later," said Medwyn. "Your friend is badly injured, you know. Come, I shall do what I can for him." He motioned for them to follow.

The wolves padded silently behind Taran, Eilonwy, and the bard. Where Melyngar waited at the end of the ravine, Medwyn lifted Gurgi from the saddle, as if the creature weighed no more than a squirrel. Gurgi lay quietly in Medwyn's arms.

The group descended a narrow footpath. Medwyn

strode ahead, as slowly and powerfully as if a tree were walking. The old man's feet were bare, but the sharp stones and pebbles did not trouble him. The path turned abruptly, then turned again. Medwyn passed through a cut in a bare shoulder of the cliff, and the next thing Taran knew, they suddenly emerged into a green, sunlit valley. Mountains, seemingly impassable, rose on all sides. Here the air was gentler, without the tooth of the wind; the grass spread rich and tender before him. Set among tall hemlocks were low, white cottages, not unlike those of Caer Dallben. At the sight of them, Taran felt a pang of homesickness. Against the face of the slope behind the cottages, he saw what appeared at first to be rows of moss-covered tree trunks; as he looked, to his surprise, they seemed more like the weather-worn ribs and timbers of a long ship. The earth covered them almost entirely; grass and meadow flowers had sprung up to obliterate them further and make them part of the mountain itself.

"I must say the old fellow's well tucked away here," whispered Fflewddur. "I could never have found the path in, and I doubt I could find the path out."

Taran nodded. The valley was the most beautiful he had ever seen. Cattle grazed peacefully in the meadow. Near the hemlocks, a small lake caught the sky and sparkled blue and white. The bright plumage of birds flashed among the trees. Even as he stepped across the lush green of the turf, Taran felt exhaustion drain from his aching body.

"There's a fawn!" Eilonwy cried with delight.

From behind the cottages, a speckled, long-legged fawn appeared, sniffed the air, then trotted quickly towards Medwyn. The graceful creature paid no attention to the wolves, but frisked gaily at the old man's side. The animal drew shyly away from the strangers; but her curiosity got the better of her, and soon she was nuzzling Eilonwy's hand.

"I've never seen a fawn this close," said the girl. "Achren never had any pets – none that would stay with her, at any rate. I can't blame them at all. This one is lovely; it makes you feel all tingly, as if you were touching the wind."

Medwyn, motioning for them to wait, carried Gurgi into the largest of cottages. The wolves sat on their haunches and watched the travellers through slanted eyes. Taran unsaddled Melyngar, who began cropping the tender grass. Half-a-dozen chickens clucked and pecked around the neat white henhouse. The rooster raised his head to show a notched comb.

"Those are Dallben's chickens!" cried Taran. "They must be! There's the brown hen, the white – I'd know that comb anywhere." He hurried over and clucked at them.

The chickens, more interested in eating, paid little attention.

Medwyn reappeared in the doorway. He carried an

enormous wicker basket laden with jugs of milk, with cheese, honeycombs, and fruits that, in the lowlands, would not be in season for another month. "I shall look after your friend directly," he said. "Meantime, I thought you might enjoy – oh, yes, so you've found them, have you?" he said, noticing Taran with the chickens. "Those are my visitors from Caer Dallben. There should be a swarm of bees, too, somewhere about."

"They flew away," Taran said, "the same day Hen Wen ran off."

"Then I imagine they came straight here," Medwyn said. "The chickens were petrified with fright; I could make no sense at all out of them. Oh, they settled down quickly enough, but of course by that time they had forgotten why they flew off in the first place. You know how chickens are, imagining the world coming to an end one moment, then pecking corn the next. They shall all fly back when they're ready, have no fear. Though it's unfortunate Dallben and Coll should be put out in the matter of eggs.

"I would ask you inside," Medwyn continued, "but the disorder at the moment – there were bears at breakfast, and you can imagine the state of things. So I must ask you to attend to yourselves. If you would rest, there is straw in the byre; it should not be too uncomfortable for you."

The travellers lost no time in helping themselves to Medwyn's provisions, or in finding the byre. The sweet

scent of hay filled the low-ceilinged building. They scooped
out nests in the straw, uncovering one of Medwyn's breakfast
guests curled up and fast asleep. Fflewddur, at first uneasy,
was finally convinced the bear had no appetite for bards,
and soon began snoring. Eilonwy dropped off to sleep in the
middle of one of her sentences.

Taran had no desire to rest. Medwyn's valley had
refreshed him more than a night's slumber. He left the byre
and strolled across the meadow. At the far side of the lake,
otters built a slide and were amusing themselves by
tumbling down it. At Taran's approach, they stopped for a
moment, raised their heads to look at him as though sorry
he was unable to join them, and returned to their game. A
fish broke water in a twinkle of silver scales; the ripples
widened until the last of them lapped gently at the shore.

Medwyn, Taran saw, had gardens of both flowers and
vegetables behind the cottage. To his surprise, Taran found
himself yearning to work with Coll in his own vegetable
plot. The weeding and hoeing he had so despised at Caer
Dallben now seemed, as he thought of his past journey and
the journey yet to come, infinitely pleasant.

He sat down by the rim of the lake and looked across
the hills. With the sun resting above the peaks, the wooden
skeleton of the great ship stood out sharply against the
mound which nearly enveloped it. He had little chance to
study it, for Medwyn appeared, walking deliberately across

the field; the fawn trotted beside him, the three wolves followed. With his brown robe and white hair, Medwyn looked as broad and solid as a snow-capped mountain.

"Gurgi is more comfortable than he was," the ancient man said in his deep voice. The fawn danced at the lake shore while Medwyn ponderously sat down and leaned his huge head towards Taran. "He will recover well; there is no longer any danger. Not, at least, while he is here."

"I have thought long of Gurgi," Taran said, looking frankly into the old man's grey eyes. He explained, then, the reason for his journey and the events leading to Gurgi's accident. Medwyn listened carefully, head cocked to one side, thoughtful, while Taran recounted Gurgi's willingness to sacrifice his own life rather than endanger the others. "At first, I wasn't too fond of him," Taran admitted. "Now I've begun to like him in spite of all his whining and complaining."

"Every living thing deserves our respect," said Medwyn, knitting his shaggy brows, "be it humble or proud, ugly or beautiful."

"I wouldn't want to say that about gwythaints," Taran answered.

"I feel only sorrow for those unhappy creatures," Medwyn said. "Once, long ago, they were as free as other birds, gentle and trusting. In his cunning, Arawn lured them to him and brought them under his power. He built the iron cages which are now their prison house in Annuvin. The tortures he inflicted on the gwythaints were shameful and unspeakable. Now they serve him out of terror.

"Thus would he strive to corrupt every animal in Prydain, no less than the race of men. That is one of the reasons I remain in the valley. Here, Arawn cannot harm them. Even so, were he to become ruler of this land, I doubt I could help them all. Those who fell into his clutches would be counted fortunate if they perished quickly."

Taran nodded. "I understand more and more why I must warn the Sons of Don. As for Gurgi, I wonder if it wouldn't be safer for him to stay here."

"Safer?" asked Medwyn. "Yes, certainly. But you would hurt him grievously were you to turn him away now. Gurgi's misfortune is that he is neither one thing nor the other, at the moment. He has lost the wisdom of animals and has not gained the learning of men. Therefore, both shun him. Were he to do something purposeful, it would mean much to him.

"I doubt he will delay your journey, for he will be able to walk as well as you – by tomorrow, easily. I urge you to take him. He may even find his own way of serving you. Neither refuse to give help when it is needed," Medwyn continued, "nor refuse to accept it when it is offered. Gwythyr Son of Greidawl learned that from a lame ant, you know."

"A lame ant?" Taran shook his head. "Dallben has taught me much about ants, but nothing of a lame one."

"It is a long history," Medwyn said, "perhaps you will hear all of it another time. For the moment, you need only know that when Kilhuch – or was it his father? No, it was young Kilhuch. Very well. When young Kilhuch sought the hand of the fair Olwen, he was given a number of tasks by her father, Yspadadden; he was the Chief Giant at the time. What the tasks were does not concern us now, except that they were nigh impossible, and Kilhuch could not have accomplished them without the aid of his companions.

"One of the tasks was to gather nine bushels of flax seed, though there was scarcely that much in all the land. For the sake of his friend, Gwythyr Son of Greidawl undertook to do this. While he was walking over the hills, wondering how he might accomplish it, he heard a grievous wailing from an anthill; a fire had started around it and the ants were in danger of their lives. Gwythyr – yes, I'm quite sure it was Gwythyr – drew his sword and beat out the fire.

"In gratitude, the ants combed every field until they had collected the nine bushels. Yet the Chief Giant, a picky and disagreeable sort, claimed the measure was not complete. One flax seed was missing, and must be delivered before nightfall.

"Gwythyr had no idea where he could find another flax seed, but at last, just as the sun had begun to set, up hobbled a lame ant carrying a heavy burden. It was the single flax seed, and so the last measure was filled.

"I have studied the race of men," Medwyn continued. "I have seen that alone you stand as weak reeds by a lake. You must learn to help yourselves, that is true; but you must also learn to help one another. Are you not, all of you, lame ants?"

Taran was silent. Medwyn put his hand into the lake and stirred the water. After a moment, a venerable salmon rippled up; Medwyn stroked the jaws of the huge fish.

"What place is this?" Taran finally asked, in a hushed voice. "Are you indeed Medwyn? You speak of the race of men as if you were not one of them."

"This is a place of peace," Medwyn said, "and therefore not suitable for men, at least, not yet. Until it is, I hold this valley for creatures of the forests and the waters. In their mortal danger they come to me, if they have the strength to do so – and in their pain and grief. Do you not believe that animals know grief and fear and pain? The world of men is not an easy one for them."

"Dallben," said Taran, "taught me that when the black waters flooded Prydain, ages ago, Nevvid Nav Neivion built a ship and carried with him two of every living creature. The waters drained away, the ship came to rest – no man knows where. But the animals who came safe again into the world remembered, and their young have never forgotten.

And here," Taran said, pointing towards the hillside, "I see a ship, far from water. Gwydion called you Medwyn, but I ask..."

"I am Medwyn," answered the white-bearded man, "for all that my name may concern you. That is not important now. My own concern is for Hen Wen."

"You have seen nothing of her, then?"

Medwyn shook his head. "What Lord Gwydion said is true: of all places in Prydain, she would have come here first, especially if she sensed her life in danger. But there has been no sign, no rumour. Yet she would find her way, sooner or later, unless..."

Taran felt a chill ripple at his heart. "Unless she has been killed," he murmured. "Do you think that has happened?"

"I do not know," Medwyn answered, "though I fear it may be so."

CHAPTER FOURTEEN

The Black Lake

That night Medwyn prepared a feast for the travellers.
The disorder left by the breakfasting bears had been
cleared away. The cottage was snug and neat, though even
smaller than Caer Dallben. Taran could see that Medwyn
was indeed unused to entertaining human visitors, for his
table was barely long enough to seat them all; and for
chairs he had been obliged to make do with benches and
milking stools.

Medwyn sat at the head of the table. The fawn had

gone to sleep, but the wolves crouched at his feet and grinned happily. On the back of his chair perched a gigantic, golden-plumed eagle, watching every movement with sharp, unblinking eyes. Fflewddur, though still apprehensive, did not allow his fear to affect his appetite. He ate enough for three, without showing the least sign of becoming full. But when he asked for another portion of venison, Medwyn gave a long chuckle and explained to the amazed Fflewddur it was not meat at all but vegetables prepared according to his own recipe.

"Of course it is," Eilonwy told the bard. "You wouldn't expect him to cook his guests, would you? That would be like asking someone to dinner and then roasting him. Really, I think bards are as muddled as Assistant Pig-Keepers; neither one of you seems to think very clearly."

As much as he welcomed food and the chance to rest, Taran was silent throughout the meal, and continued so when he retired to his nest of straw. Until now, he had never imagined Hen Wen might not be alive. He had spoken again with Medwyn, but the old man could give him no assurance.

Wakeful, Taran left the byre and stood outside, looking at the sky. In the clear air, the stars were blue-white, closer than he had ever seen them. He tried to turn his thoughts from Hen Wen; reaching Caer Dathyl was the task he had undertaken and that in itself would be difficult enough. An owl passed overhead, silent as ashes. The shadow appearing noiselessly beside him was Medwyn.

"Not asleep?" Medwyn asked. "A restless night is no way to begin a journey."

"It is a journey I am eager to end," Taran said. "There are times when I fear I shall not see Caer Dallben again."

"It is not given to men to know the ends of their journeys," Medwyn answered. "It may be that you will never return to the places dearest to you. But how can that matter, if what you must do is here and now?"

"I think," said Taran longingly, "that if I knew I were not to see my own home again, I would be happy to stay in this valley."

"Your heart is young and unformed," Medwyn said. "Yet, if I read it well, you are of the few I would welcome here. Indeed, you may stay if you choose. Surely you can entrust your task to your friends."

"No," said Taran, after a long pause, "I have taken it on myself through my own choice."

"If that is so," answered Medwyn, "then you can give it up through your own choice."

From all over the valley it seemed to Taran there came voices urging him to remain. The hemlocks whispered of rest and peace; the lake spoke of sunlight lingering in its depths, the joy of otters at their games. He turned away.

"No," he said quickly, "my decision was made long before this."

"Then," Medwyn answered gently, "so be it." He put a hand on Taran's brow. "I grant you all that you will allow me to grant: a night's rest. Sleep well."

Taran remembered nothing of returning to the byre or falling asleep, but he rose in the morning sunlight refreshed and strengthened. Eilonwy and the bard had already finished their breakfast, and Taran was delighted to see that Gurgi had joined them. As Taran approached, Gurgi gave a yelp of joy and turned gleeful somersaults.

"Oh, joy!" he cried. "Gurgi is ready for new walkings and stalkings, oh, yes! And new seekings and peekings! Great lords have been kind to happy, jolly Gurgi!"

Taran noticed Medwyn had not only healed the creature's leg, he had also given him a bath and a good combing. Gurgi looked only half as twiggy and leafy as usual. In addition, as he saddled Melyngar, Taran found that Medwyn had packed the saddlebags with food, and had included warm cloaks for all of them.

The old man called the travellers around him and seated himself on the ground. "The armies of the Horned King are by now a day's march ahead of you," he said, "but if you follow the paths I shall reveal, and move quickly, you may regain the time you have lost. It is even possible for you to reach Caer Dathyl a day, perhaps two, before them.

However, I warn you, the mountain ways are not easy. If you prefer, I shall set you on a path towards the Valley of Ystrad once again."

"Then we would be following the Horned King," Taran said. "There would be less chance of overtaking him, and much danger, too."

"Do not think the mountains are not dangerous," Medwyn said. "Though it is a danger of a different sort."

"A Fflam thrives on danger!" cried the bard. "Let it be the mountains or the Horned King's hosts, I fear neither — not to any great extent," he added quickly.

"We shall risk the mountains," Taran said.

"For once," Eilonwy interrupted, "you've decided the right thing. The mountains certainly aren't going to throw spears at us, no matter how dangerous they are. I really think you're improving."

"Listen carefully, then," Medwyn ordered. As he spoke, his hands moved deftly in the soft earth before him, moulding a tiny model of hills, which Taran found easier to follow than Fflewddur's map scratchings. When he finished, and the travellers' gear and weapons were secured on Melyngar's back, Medwyn led the group from the valley. As closely as Taran observed each step of the way, he knew the path to Medwyn's valley would be lost to him as soon as the ancient man left.

In a little while Medwyn stopped. "Your path now lies

to the north," he said, "and here we shall part. And you, Taran of Caer Dallben – whether you have chosen wisely, you will learn from your own heart. Perhaps we shall meet again, and you will tell me. Until then, farewell."

Before Taran could turn and thank Medwyn, the white-bearded man disappeared, as if the hills had swallowed him up; and the travellers stood by themselves on a rocky, windswept plateau.

"Well," said Fflewddur, hitching up the harp behind him, "I somehow feel that if we meet any more wolves, they'll know we're friends of Medwyn."

The first day's march was less difficult than Taran had feared. This time, he led the way, for the bard admitted – after a number of harp strings had snapped – that he had not been able to keep all Medwyn's directions in his head.

They climbed steadily until long after the sun had turned westwards; and, though the ground was rough and broken, the path Medwyn had indicated lay clearly before them. Mountain streams, whose water ran cold and clear, made winding lines of sparkling silver as they danced down the slopes into the distant valley lands. The air was bracing, yet with a cold edge which made the travellers grateful for the cloaks Medwyn had given them.

At a long cleft protected from the wind, Taran signalled a halt. They had made excellent progress during the day, far more than he had expected, and he saw no reason to exhaust themselves by forcing a march during the night. Tethering Melyngar to one of the stunted trees that grew in the heights, the travellers made camp. Since there was no further danger from the Cauldron Born, and the hosts of the Horned King moved far below and to the west of the group, Taran deemed it safe to build a fire. Medwyn's provisions needed no cooking, but the blaze warmed and cheered them. As the night shadows drifted from the peaks, Eilonwy lit her golden sphere and set it in the crevice of a faulted rock.

Gurgi, who had not uttered a single moan or groan during this part of the journey, perched on a boulder and began scratching himself luxuriously; although, after Medwyn's washing and combing, it was more through habit than anything else. The bard, as lean as ever, despite the huge amount he had eaten, repaired his harp strings.

"You've been carrying that harp ever since I met you," Eilonwy said, "and you've never once played it. That's like telling somebody you want to talk to them, and when they get ready to listen, you don't say anything."

"You'd hardly expect me to go strumming out airs while those Cauldron warriors were following us," Fflewddur said. "Somehow I didn't think it would be appropriate. But –

a Fflam is always obliging, so if you really care to hear me play..." he added, looking both delighted and embarrassed. He cradled the instrument in one arm and, almost before his fingers touched the strings, a gentle melody, as beautiful as the curve of the harp itself, lifted like a voice singing without words.

To Taran's ear, the melody had its own words, weaving a supple thread among the rising notes. Home, home, they sang; and beyond the words themselves, so fleeting he could not be quite sure of them, were the fields and orchards of Caer Dallben, the gold afternoons of autumn and the crisp winter mornings with pink sunlight on the snow.

Then the harp fell silent. Fflewddur sat with his head bent close to the strings, a curious expression on his long face. "Well, that was a surprise," said the bard at last. "I had planned something a little more lively, the sort of thing my war-leader always enjoys — to put us in a bold frame of mind, you understand. The truth of the matter is," he admitted with a slight tone of discouragement, "I don't really know what's going to come out of it next. My fingers go along, but sometimes I think this harp plays of itself.

"Perhaps," Fflewddur continued, "that's why Taliesin thought he was doing me a favour when he gave it to me. Because when I went up to the Council of Bards for my examination, I had an old pot one of the minstrels had left behind and I couldn't do more than plunk out a few chants. However, a Fflam never looks a gift horse in the mouth, or, in this case, I should say harp."

"It was a sad tune," Eilonwy said. "But the odd thing about it is, you don't mind the sadness. It's like feeling better after you've had a good cry. It made me think of the sea again, though I haven't been there since I was a little girl." At this, Taran snorted, but Eilonwy paid no attention to him. "The waves break against the cliffs and churn into foam, and farther out, as far as you can see, there are the white crests, the White Horses of Llyr, they call them; but they're really only waves waiting their turn to roll in."

"Strange," said the bard, "personally, I was thinking of my own castle. It's small and draughty, but I would like to see it again; a person can have enough wandering, you know. It made me think I might even settle down again and try to be a respectable sort of king."

"Caer Dallben is closer to my heart," Taran said. "When I left, I never gave it too much thought. Now I think of it a great deal."

Gurgi, who had been listening silently, set up a long howl. "Yes, yes, soon great warriors will all be back in their halls, telling their tales with laughings and chaffings. Then it will be the fearful forest again for poor Gurgi, to put down his tender head in snoozings and snorings."

"Gurgi," Taran said, "I promise to bring you to Caer Dallben, if I ever get there myself. And if you like it, and Dallben agrees, you can stay there as long as you want."

"What joy!" Gurgi cried. "Honest, toiling Gurgi extends thanks and best wishes. Oh, yes, fond, obedient Gurgi will work hard..."

"For now, obedient Gurgi had better sleep," Taran advised, "and so should we all. Medwyn has put us well on our way, and it can't take much longer. We'll start again at daybreak."

During the night, however, a gale rose, and by morning a drenching rain beat into the cleft. Instead of slackening, the wind gained in force and screamed over the rocks. It beat like a fist against the travellers' shelter, then pried with searching fingers, as if to seize and dash them into the valley.

They set out nevertheless, holding their cloaks before their faces. To make matters worse, the path broke off entirely and sheer cliffs loomed ahead of them. The rain stopped, after the travellers had all been soaked to the skin, but now the rocks were slippery and treacherous. Even the surefooted Melyngar stumbled once, and for a breathless moment Taran feared she would be lost.

The mountains swung a half-circle around a lake black and sullen below threatening clouds. Taran halted on an outcropping of stone and pointed towards the hills at the far side of the lake. "According to what Medwyn told us," he said to the bard, "we should make for that notch, all the way over there. But I see no purpose in following the mountains when we can cut almost straight across. The lake shore is flat, at least, while here it's getting practically impossible to climb."

Fflewddur rubbed his pointed nose. "Even counting the time it would take us to go down and come back up again, I think we should save several hours. Yes, I definitely believe it's worth trying."

"Medwyn didn't say a word about crossing valleys," Eilonwy put in.

"He didn't say anything about cliffs like these," answered Taran. "They seem nothing to him; he's lived here a long time. For us, it's something else again."

"If you don't listen to what somebody tells you," Eilonwy remarked, "it's like putting your fingers in your ears and jumping down a well. For an Assistant Pig-Keeper who's done very little travelling, you suddenly know all about it."

"Who found the way out of the barrow?" Taran retorted. "It's decided. We cross the valley."

The descent was laborious, but once they had reached

ground level, Taran felt all the more convinced they would save time. Holding Melyngar's bridle, he led the group along the narrow shore. The lake reached closely to the base of the hills, obliging Taran to splash through the shallows. The lake, he realized, was not black in reflection of the sky; the water itself was dark, flat, and as grim and heavy as iron. The bottom, too, was as treacherous as the rocks above. Despite his care, Taran lurched and nearly got a ducking. When he turned to warn the others, to his surprise he saw Gurgi in water up to his waist and heading towards the centre of the lake. Fflewddur and Eilonwy were also splashing farther and farther from land.

"Don't go through the water," Taran called. "Keep to the shore!"

"Wish we could," the bard shouted back. "But we're stuck somehow. There's a terribly strong pull..."

A moment later, Taran understood what the bard meant. An unexpected swell knocked him off his feet and even as he put out his hands to break his fall the black lake sucked him down. Beside him, Melyngar thrashed her legs and whinnied. The sky spun overhead. He was pulled along like a twig in a torrent. Eilonwy shot past him. He tried to regain his footing and catch her. It was too late. He skimmed and bobbed over the surface. The far shore would stop them, Taran thought, struggling to keep his head above the waves. A roar filled his ears. The middle of the lake was a whirlpool clutching and flinging him to the depths. Black water closed over him, and he knew he was drowning.

CHAPTER FIFTEEN

King Eiddileg

Down he spun, battling for air, in a flood that broke upon him like a crumbling mountain. Faster and faster the waters bore him along, tossing him right and left. Taran collided with something – what it was, he could not tell – but he clung to it even as his strength failed him. There was a crash, as though the earth had split asunder; the water turned to foam, and Taran felt himself dashed against an unyielding wall. He remembered nothing more.

When he opened his eyes he was lying on a hard,

smooth surface, his hand tightly gripping Fflewddur's harp. He heard the rush of water close by. Cautiously, he felt around him; his fingers touched only wet, flat stone, an embankment of some kind. A pale blue light shone high above him. Taran decided he had come to rest in a cave or grotto. He raised himself and his movement set the harp to jangling.

"Hello! Who's that?" A voice echoed down the embankment. Faint though it was, Taran recognized it as belonging to the bard. He scrambled to his feet and crept in the direction of the sound. On the way he tripped over a form, which became suddenly vocal and indignant.

"You've done very well, Taran of Caer Dallben, with all your short cuts. What's left of me is soaked to the skin, and I can't find my bauble – oh, here it is, all wet, of course. And who knows what's happened to the rest of us?"

The golden light flared dimly to reveal the dripping face of Eilonwy, her blue eyes flashing with vexation.

Gurgi's hairy, sputtering shadow rolled towards them. "Oh, poor tender head is filled with sloshings and washings!"

In another moment Fflewddur had found them. Melyngar whinnied behind him. "I thought I heard my harp down here," he said. "I couldn't believe it at first. Never expected to see it again. But – a Fflam never despairs! Quite a stroke of luck, though."

"I never thought I'd see anything again," Taran said, handing the instrument to Fflewddur. "We've been washed into a cave of some kind; but it's not a natural one. Look at these flagstones."

"If you'd look at Melyngar," Eilonwy called, "you'd see all our provisions are gone. All our weapons, too, thanks to your precious short cut!"

It was true. The straps had broken loose and the saddle had torn away in the whirlpool. Luckily, the companions still had their swords.

"I'm sorry," Taran said. "I admit we are here through my fault. I should not have followed this path, but what's done is done. I led us here, and I'll find a way out."

He glanced around. The roar of water came from a wide, swift-running canal. The embankment itself was much broader than he had realized. Lights of various colours glowed in the high arches. He turned to his companions again. "This is very curious. We seem to be deep underground, but it isn't the lake bottom – "

Before he could utter another word, he was seized from behind, and a bag smelling strongly of onions was jammed over his head. Eilonwy screamed, then her voice grew muffled. Taran was being half-pushed, half-pulled in two directions at once. Gurgi began yelping furiously.

"Here! Get that one!" a gruff voice shouted.

"Get him yourself! Can't you see I've got my hands full?"

Taran struck out. A solid, round ball that must have been someone's head butted him in the stomach. There were slapping noises filtering through the oniony darkness around him. Those would be from Eilonwy. Now he was pushed from behind, propelled at top speed, while angry voices shouted at him – and at each other. "Hustle along there!"

"You fool, you didn't take their swords!" – At this, came another shriek from Eilonwy, the sound of what might have been a kick, then a moment of silence – "All right, let them keep their swords. You'll have the blame of it, letting them approach King Eiddileg with weapons!"

At a blind trot, Taran was shoved through what seemed a large crowd of people. Everyone was talking at once; the noise was deafening. After a number of turns, he was thrust forwards again. A heavy door snapped behind him; the onion bag was snatched from his head.

Taran blinked. With Fflewddur and Eilonwy he stood in the centre of a high-vaulted chamber, glittering with lights. Gurgi was nowhere in sight. Their captors were half-a-dozen squat, round, stubby-legged warriors. Axes hung from their belts and each man had a bow and quiver of arrows on his shoulder. The left eye of the short, burly fellow who stood beside Eilonwy was turning greenish black.

Before them, at a long stone table, a dwarfish figure with a bristling yellow beard glared at the warriors. He wore a robe of garish red and green. Rings sparkled on his plump fingers. "What's this?" he shouted. "Who are these people? Didn't I give orders I wasn't to be disturbed?"

"But Majesty," began one of the warriors, shifting uneasily, "we caught them..."

"*Must* you bother me with details?" King Eiddileg cried, clasping his forehead. "You'll ruin me! You'll be the death of me! Out! Out! No, not the *prisoners*, you idiots!" Shaking his head, sighing and sputtering, the King collapsed onto a throne carved from rock. The guards scurried away. King Eiddileg shot a furious glance at Taran and his companions. "Now, then, out with it. What do you want? You might as well know ahead of time, you shan't have it."

"Sire," Taran began, "we ask no more than safe passage through the realm. The four of us..."

"There's only three of you," King Eiddileg snapped. "Can't you count?"

"One of my companions is missing," Taran said regretfully. He had hoped Gurgi would have overcome his fear, but he could not blame the creature for running off after his ordeal in the whirlpool. "I beg your servants to help us find him. Then, too, our provisions and weapons have been lost..."

"That's clotted nonsense!" shouted the King. "Don't lie to me, I can't stand it." He pulled an orange kerchief from his sleeve and mopped his forehead. "Why did you come here?"

"Because an Assistant Pig-Keeper led us on a wild-goose chase," Eilonwy interrupted. "We don't even know *where* we are, let alone why. It's worse than rolling downhill in the dark."

"Naturally," said Eiddileg, his voice dripping with sarcasm. "You have no idea you're in the very heart of the Kingdom of Tylwyth Teg, the Fair Folk, the Happy Family, the Little People, or whatever other insipid, irritating names you've put on us. Oh, no, of course not. You just happened to be passing by."

"We were caught in the lake," Taran protested. "It pulled us down."

"Good, eh?" King Eiddileg answered, with a quick smile of pride. "I've added some improvements of my own, of course."

"If you're so anxious to keep visitors away," Eilonwy said, "you should have something better — to make people stay *out*."

"When people get this close," Eiddileg answered, "they're already *too* close. At that point, I don't want them out, I want them *in*."

Fflewddur shook his head. "I always understood the

Fair Folk were all over Prydain, not just here."

"Of course, not just here," said Eiddileg with impatience. "This is the royal seat. Why, we have tunnels and mines every place you can imagine. But the real work – the real labour of organization – is here, right here, in this very spot – in this very throne room. On my shoulders! It's too much, I tell you, too much. But who else can you trust? If you want something done right..." The King stopped suddenly and drummed his glittering fingers on the stone table. "That's not your affair," he said. "You're in trouble enough as it is. It can't be overlooked."

"*I* don't see any work being done," said Eilonwy.

Before Taran could warn Eilonwy not to be imprudent, the door of the throne room burst open and a crowd of folk pressed in. Looking closer, Taran saw not all were dwarfs; some were tall, slender, with white robes; others were covered with glistening scales, like fish; still others fluttered large, delicate wings. For some moments Taran heard nothing but a confusion of voices, angry outcries and bickering, with Eiddileg trying to shout above them. Finally, the King managed to push them all out again. "No work being done?" he cried. "You don't appreciate everything that goes into it. The Children of Evening – that's another ridiculous name you humans have thought up – are to sing in the forest of Cantrev Mawr tonight. They haven't even practised. Two are sick and one can't be found.

"The Lake Sprites have been quarrelling all day; now they're sulking. Their hair's a mess. And who does that reflect on? Who has to jolly them along, coax them, plead with them? The answer is obvious.

"What thanks do I get for it?" King Eiddileg ranted on. "None at all! Has any of you long-legged gawks ever taken the trouble – even once, mind you – to offer the simplest expression of gratitude, such as, 'Thank you, King Eiddileg, for the tremendous effort and inconvenience you've gone to, so that we can enjoy a little charm and beauty in the world above, which would be so unspeakably grim without you and your Fair Folk'? Just a few words of honest appreciation?

"By no means! Just the opposite! If any of you thick-skulled oafs come on one of the Fair Folk above ground, what happens? You seize him! You grab him with your great hammy hands and try to make him lead you to buried treasure. Or you squeeze him until you get three wishes out of him – not satisfied with one, oh, no, but *three*!

"Well, I don't mind telling you this," Eiddileg went on, his face turning redder by the moment, "I've put an end to all this wish-granting and treasure-scavenging. No more! Absolutely not! I'm surprised you didn't ruin us long ago!"

Just then a chorus of voices rose from behind the door of Eiddileg's throne room. The harmonies penetrated even the walls of heavy stone. Taran had never in his life heard such beautiful singing. He listened, enchanted, forgetting, for the moment, all but the soaring melody. Eiddileg himself stopped shouting and puffing until the voices died away.

"That's something to be thankful for," the King said at last. "The Children of Evening have evidently got together again. Not as good as you might want, but they'll manage somehow."

"I have not heard the songs of the Fair Folk until now," Taran said. "I had never realized how lovely they were."

"Don't try to flatter me," Eiddileg cried, trying to look furious, yet beaming at the same time.

"What surprises me," Eilonwy said, while the bard plucked meditatively at his harp, trying to recapture the notes of the song, "is why you go to so much trouble. If you Fair Folk dislike all of us above ground, why do you bother?"

"Professional pride, my dear girl," said the Dwarf King, putting a chubby hand to his heart and bowing slightly. "When we Fair Folk do something, we do it right. Oh, yes," he sighed, "never mind the sacrifices we make. It's a task that needs doing, and so we do it. Never mind the cost. For myself," he added, with a wave of his hand, "it doesn't matter. I've lost sleep, I've lost weight, but that's not important..."

If King Eiddileg had lost weight, Taran thought to himself, what must he have been like beforehand? He decided against asking this question.

"Well, *I* appreciate it," Eilonwy said. "I think it's amazing what you've been able to do. You must be extremely clever, and any Assistant Pig-Keepers who happen to be in this throne room might do well to pay attention."

"Thank you, dear girl," said King Eiddileg, bowing lower. "I see you're the sort of person one can talk to intelligently. It's unheard of for one of you big shambling louts to have any kind of insight into these matters. But you at least seem to understand the problems we face."

"Sire," interrupted Taran, "we understand your time is precious. Let us disturb you no more. Give us safe conduct to Caer Dathyl."

"What?" shouted Eiddileg. "Leave here? Impossible! Unheard of! Once you're with the Fair Folk, my good lad, you *stay*, and no mistake about it. Oh, I suppose I could stretch a point, for the sake of the young lady, and let you off easily. Only put you to sleep for fifty years, or turn you all into bats; but that would be a pure favour, mind you."

"Our task is urgent," Taran cried. "Even now we have delayed too long."

"That's your concern, not mine." Eiddileg shrugged.

"Then we shall make our own way," Taran shouted, drawing his sword. Fflewddur's blade leaped out and the bard stood with Taran, ready to fight.

"More clotted nonsense," King Eiddileg said, looking contemptuously at the swords pointing towards him. He shook his fingers at them. "There! And there! Now you might try to move your arms."

Taran strained every muscle. His body felt turned to stone.

"Put your swords away and let's talk this over calmly," said the Dwarf King, gesturing again. "If you give me any decent reason why I should let you go, I might think it over and answer you promptly, say in a year or two."

There could be no use, Taran saw, in concealing the reasons for his journey; he explained to Eiddileg what had befallen them. The Dwarf King ceased his blustering at the mention of Arawn, but when Taran had finished, King Eiddileg shook his head.

"This is a conflict you great gawks must attend to yourselves. The Fair Folk owe you no allegiance," he said angrily. "Prydain belonged to us before the race of men came. *You* drove us underground. You plundered our mines, you blundering codpoles! You stole our treasures, and you keep on stealing them, you clumsy oafs..."

"Sire," Taran answered, "I can speak for no man but myself. I have never robbed you and I have no wish to. My task means more to me than your treasures. If there is ill will between the Fair Folk and the race of men, then it is a matter to be settled between them. But if the Horned King triumphs, if the shadow of Annuvin falls on the land above you, Arawn's hand will reach your deepest caverns."

"For an Assistant Pig-Keeper," said Eiddileg, "you're reasonably eloquent. But the Fair Folk will worry about Arawn when the time comes."

"The time has come," Taran said. "I only hope it has not passed."

"I don't think you really know what's going on above ground," Eilonwy suddenly exclaimed. "You talk about charm and beauty and sacrificing yourself to make things pleasant for people. I don't believe you care a bit for that. You're too conceited and stubborn and selfish..."

"Conceited!" shouted Eiddileg, his eyes popping. "Selfish! You won't find anyone more open-hearted and generous. How dare you say that? What do you want, my life's blood?" With that, he tore off his cloak and threw it in the air, pulled the rings from his fingers and tossed them in every direction. "Go ahead! Take it all! Leave me ruined! What else do you want — my whole kingdom? Do you want to leave? Go, by all means. The sooner the better! Stubborn? I'm too soft! It will be the death of me! But little you care!"

At that moment the door of the throne room burst open again. Two dwarf warriors clung frantically to Gurgi, who swung them about as if they were rabbits.

"Joyous greetings! Faithful Gurgi is back with mighty heroes! This time valiant Gurgi did not run! Oh, no, no! Brave Gurgi fought with great whackings and smackings.

He triumphed! But then, mighty lords are carried away. Clever Gurgi goes seeking and peeking to save them, yes! And he finds them!

"But that is not all. Oh, faithful, honest, fearless Gurgi finds more. Surprises and delights, oh, joy!" Gurgi was so excited that he began dancing on one foot, spinning around and clapping his hands.

"Mighty warriors go seek a piggy! It is clever, wise Gurgi who finds her!"

"Hen Wen?" cried Taran. "Where is she?"

"Here, mighty lord," Gurgi shouted, "the piggy is here!"

CHAPTER SIXTEEN

Doli

Taran turned accusingly to King Eiddileg. "You said nothing of Hen Wen."

"You didn't ask me," said Eiddileg.

"That's sharp practice," Fflewddur muttered, "even for a king."

"It's worse than a lie," Taran said angrily. "You'd have let us go our way, and we'd never have known what happened to her."

"You should be ashamed of yourself," Eilonwy put in,

179

shaking her finger at the King, who appeared most embarrassed at being found out. "It's like looking the other way when someone's about to walk into a hole."

"Finders keepers," the Dwarf King snapped. "A troop of the Fair Folk came on her near the Avren banks. She was running through a ravine. And I'll tell you something you don't know. Half a dozen warriors were after her, the henchmen of the Horned King. The troop took care of those warriors — we have our own ways of dealing with you clumsy lummoxes — and they brought your pig here, underground most of the way."

"No wonder Gwydion could find no tracks," Taran murmured to himself.

"The Fair Folk rescued her," Eiddileg angrily continued, turning bright red, "and there's another fine example. Do I get a word of thanks? Naturally not. But I do get called disagreeable names and have nasty thoughts thrown at me. Oh, I can see it in your faces. Eiddileg is a thief and a wretch — that's what you're saying to yourselves. Well, just for that you shan't have her back. And you'll stay here, all of you, until I feel like letting you go."

Eilonwy gasped with indignation. "If you do that," she cried, "you *are* a thief and a wretch! You gave me your word. The Fair Folk don't go back on their word."

"There was no mention of a pig, no mention at all."

Eiddileg clapped his hands over his paunch and snapped his mouth shut.

"No," Taran said, "there was not. But there is a question of honesty and honour."

Eiddileg blinked and looked sideways. He took out his orange kerchief and mopped his brow again. "Honour," he muttered, "yes, I was afraid you'd come to that. True, the Fair Folk never break their word. Well," he sighed, "that's the price for being openhearted and generous. So be it. You shall have your pig."

"We shall need weapons to replace those we lost," Taran said.

"What?" screamed Eiddileg. "Are you trying to ruin me?"

"And crunchings and munchings!" piped up Gurgi.

Taran nodded. "Provisions, as well."

"This is going too far," Eiddileg shouted. "You're bleeding me to death! Weapons! Food! Pigs!"

"And we beg for a guide who will show us the way to Caer Dathyl."

At this, Eiddileg nearly exploded. When finally he calmed himself, he nodded reluctantly. "I shall lend you Doli," he said. "He is the only one I can spare." He clapped his hands and gave orders to the armed dwarfs, then turned to the companions.

"Off with you now, before I change my mind."

Eilonwy stepped quickly to the throne, bent and kissed Eiddileg on the top of his head. "Thank you," she whispered, "you're a perfectly lovely king."

"Out! Out!" the dwarf cried. As the stone door closed behind him, Taran saw King Eiddileg fondling his head and beaming happily.

The troop of Fair Folk led the company down the vaulted corridors. Taran had at first imagined Eiddileg's realm to be no more than a maze of underground galleries. To his astonishment, the corridors soon broadened into wide avenues. In the great domes far overhead, gems glittered as bright as sunshine. There was no grass, but deep carpets of green lichen stretched out like meadows. There were blue lakes, glistening as much as the jewels above; and cottages, and small farmhouses. It was difficult for Taran and his companions to realize they were underground.

"I've been thinking," whispered Fflewddur, "that it might be wiser to leave Hen Wen here, until we can return for her."

"I thought of that, too," answered Taran. "It's not that I don't trust Eiddileg to keep his word – most of the time. But I'm not sure we should take another chance in that lake, and I doubt we could find another way into his kingdom. He certainly won't make it easy for us to come back, I'm afraid. No, we must take Hen Wen while we have the chance. Once she's with me again, I won't let her out of my sight."

Suddenly the Fair Folk halted at one of the cottages, and from a neatly carpentered pen Taran head a loud "Hwoinch!"

He raced to the sty. Hen Wen was standing with her front feet on the rails, grunting at the top of her voice.

One of the Fair Folk opened the gate and the white pig burst out, wriggling and squealing.

Taran threw his arms around Hen Wen's neck. "Oh, Hen!" he cried. "Even Medwyn thought you were dead!"

"Hwch! Hwaaw!" Hen Wen chuckled joyfully. Her beady eyes sparkled. With her great pink snout she rooted affectionately under Taran's chin and came close to knocking him down.

"She looks like a wonderful pig," Eilonwy said, scratching Hen Wen behind the ears. "It's always nice to see two friends meet again. It's like waking up with the sun shining."

"She's certainly a great deal of pig," agreed the bard, "though very handsome, I must say."

"And clever, noble, brave, wise Gurgi found her."

"Have no fear," Taran said with a smile to Gurgi, "there's no chance we'll forget it."

Rolling and waddling on her short legs, Hen Wen followed Taran happily, while the Fair Folk proceeded across the fields to where a stocky figure waited. The captain of the troop announced that this was Doli, the guide Eiddileg had promised. Doli, short and stumpy, almost as broad as he was tall, wore a rust-coloured leather jacket and stout, knee-high boots. A round cap covered his head, but not enough to conceal a fringe of flaming red hair. An axe and short sword hung from his belt; and over his shoulder, he wore the stubby bow of the Fair Folk warrior.

Taran bowed politely. The dwarf stared at him with a pair of bright red eyes and snorted. Then, to Taran's surprise, Doli took a deep breath and held it until his face turned scarlet and he looked about to burst. After a few moments, the dwarf puffed out his cheeks and snorted again.

"What's the trouble?" asked Taran.

"You can still see me, can't you?" Doli burst out angrily.

"Of course, I can still see you." Taran frowned. "Why shouldn't I?"

Doli gave him a scornful look and did not answer.

Two of the Fair Folk led up Melyngar. King Eiddileg, Taran saw with relief, was as good as his word. The saddlebags bulged with provisions, and the white mare also carried a number of spears, bows, and arrows — short and heavy, as were all the weapons of the Fair Folk, but carefully and sturdily crafted.

Without another word, Doli beckoned them to follow him across the meadow. Grumbling and muttering to himself, the dwarf led them to what seemed to be the sheer face of a cliff. Only after he had reached it did Taran see long flights of steps carved into the living rock. Doli jerked his head towards the stairway and they began to climb.

This passageway of the Fair Folk was steeper than any of the mountains they had crossed. Melyngar strained forwards. Wheezing and gasping, Hen Wen pulled herself up each step. The stairway turned and twisted; at one point, the darkness was such that the companions lost sight of each other. After a time, the steps broke off and the group trod a narrow pathway of hard-packed stones. Sheets of white light rippled ahead and the travellers found themselves behind a high waterfall. One after the other, they leaped the glistening rocks, splashed through the foaming stream, and at last emerged into the cool air of the hills.

Doli squinted up at the sun. "Not much daylight left," he muttered, more gruffly than King Eiddileg himself. "Don't think I'm going to walk my legs off all night, either. Didn't ask for this work, you know. Got picked for it. Guiding a crew of – of what! An Assistant Pig-Keeper. A yellow-headed idiot with a harp. A girl with a sword. A shaggy what-is-it. Not to mention the livestock. All you can hope for is you don't run into a real war band. They'd do for you, they would. There's not one of you looks as if he could handle a blade. Humph!"

This was the most Doli had spoken since they had left

Eiddileg's realm and, despite the dwarf's uncomplimentary opinions, Taran hoped he would finally come around to being civil. Doli, however, had said all he intended to say for a while; later, when Taran ventured to speak to him, the dwarf turned angrily away and started holding his breath again.

"For goodness' sake," Eilonwy cried, "I wish you'd stop that. It makes me feel as if I'd drunk too much water, just watching you."

"It still doesn't work," Doli growled.

"Whatever are you trying to do?" Taran asked.

Even Hen Wen stared curiously at the dwarf.

"What does it look like?" Doli answered. "I'm trying to make myself invisible."

"That's an odd thing to attempt," remarked Fflewddur.

"I'm *supposed* to be invisible," snapped Doli. "My whole family can do it. Just like that! Like blowing out a candle. But not me. No wonder they all laugh at me. No wonder Eiddileg sends me out with a pack of fools. If there's anything nasty or disagreeable to be done, it's always 'find good old Doli'. If there's gems to be cut or blades to be decorated or arrows to be footed – that's the job for good old Doli!"

The dwarf held his breath again, this time so long that his face turned blue and his ears trembled.

"I think you're getting it now," said the bard, with an

encouraging smile. "I can't see you at all." No sooner had this remark passed his lips than a harp string snapped in two. Fflewddur looked sorrowfully at the instrument. "Blast the thing," he muttered, "I knew I was exaggerating somewhat; I only did it to make him feel better. He actually did seem to be fading a bit around the edges."

"If I could carve gems and do all those other things," Taran remarked sympathetically to Doli, "I wouldn't mind not being invisible. All I know is vegetables and horseshoes, and not too much about that either."

"It's silly," Eilonwy added, "to worry because you can't do something you simply can't do. That's worse than trying to make yourself taller by standing on your head."

None of these well-intentioned remarks cheered the dwarf, who strode angrily ahead, swinging his axe from side to side. Despite his bad temper, Doli was an excellent guide, Taran realized. Most of the time, the dwarf said little beyond his usual grunts and snorts, making no attempt to explain the path he followed or to suggest how long it would take the companions to reach Caer Dathyl. Taran, nevertheless, had learned a great deal of woodcraft and tracking during his journey, and he was aware the companions had begun turning westwards to descend the hills. They had, during the afternoon, covered more ground than Taran thought possible, and he knew it was thanks to Doli's expert guidance. When he congratulated the dwarf,

Doli answered only, "Humph!" — and held his breath.

They camped that night on the sheltered slope of the last barrier of mountains. Gurgi, whom Taran had taught to build a fire, was delighted to be useful; he cheerfully gathered twigs, dug a cooking pit, and, to the surprise of all, distributed the provisions equally without saving out a private share for his own crunchings and munchings later on.

Doli refused to do anything whatsoever. He took his own food from a large leather wallet hanging at his side, and sat on a rock, chewing glumly; he snorted with annoyance between every mouthful, and occasionally held his breath.

"Keep at it, old boy!" called Fflewddur. "Another try might do it! Your outline looks definitely blurred."

"Oh, hush!" Eilonwy told the bard. "Don't encourage him or he'll decide to hold his breath for ever."

"Just lending support," explained the crestfallen bard. "A Fflam never gives up, and I don't see why a dwarf should."

Hen Wen had not left Taran's side all day. Now, as he spread his cloak on the ground, the white pig grunted with pleasure, waddled over, and hunkered down beside him. Her crinkled ears relaxed; she thrust her snout comfortably against Taran's shoulder and chuckled contentedly, a blissful smile on her face. Soon the whole weight of her head pressed on him, making it impossible for Taran to roll onto his side. Hen Wen snored luxuriously and Taran resigned himself to sleeping, despite the assortment of whistles and groans directly below his ear. "I'm glad to see you, Hen," he said, "and I'm glad you're glad to see me. But I wish you wouldn't be so loud about it."

Next morning they turned their backs on the Eagle Mountains and began heading for what Taran hoped would be Caer Dathyl. As the trees rose more densely around them, Taran turned for a last glimpse of the Eagle itself, tall and serene in the distance. He was grateful their path had not led them over it, but in his heart he hoped one day to return and climb its towers of sun-flecked ice and black stone. Until this journey, he had never seen mountains, but now he understood why Gwydion had spoken longingly of Caer Dathyl.

His thought led Taran to wonder again what else Gwydion had expected to learn from Hen Wen. When they halted, he spoke to Fflewddur about it.

"There may be someone in Caer Dathyl who can understand her," Taran said. "But if we could only get her to prophesy now, she might tell us something important."

The bard agreed; however, as Taran had pointed out, they had no letter sticks.

"I could try a new spell," offered Eilonwy. "Achren

taught me some others, but I don't know if they'd be any use. They haven't anything to do with oracular pigs. I do know a wonderful one for summoning toads. Achren was about to teach me the spell for opening locks, but I don't suppose I'll ever learn it now. Even so, locks haven't much to do with pigs, either."

Eilonwy kneeled beside Hen Wen and whispered rapidly. Hen Wen seemed to listen politely for a while, grinning broadly, wheezing, and snuffling. She gave no sign of understanding a word of what the girl was saying; and at last, with a joyful "Hwoinch!" she broke away and ran to Taran, wriggling gleefully.

"It's no use," Taran said, "and there's no sense in losing time. I hope they have letter sticks in Caer Dathyl. Though I doubt it. Whatever Dallben has, it seems to be the only one of its kind in all Prydain."

They resumed their march. Gurgi, now official cook and firemaker, strode boldly behind the dwarf. Doli led the companions through a clearing and past a line of alders. A few moments later the dwarf halted and cocked his head.

Taran heard a sound, too: a faint, high-pitched screaming. It seemed to come from a twisted thornbush. Drawing his sword, Taran hurried past the dwarf. At first he could see nothing in the dark tangle. He drew closer, then stopped abruptly.

It was a gwythaint.

CHAPTER SEVENTEEN

The Fledgling

The gwythaint hung like a crumpled black rag, one wing upraised, the other folded awkwardly on its breast. No larger than a raven, it was young and barely out of its first moult; the head seemed a little too big for its body, the feathers thin and quilly. As Taran cautiously approached, the gwythaint fluttered vainly, unable to free itself. The bird opened its curved beak and hissed warningly; but its eyes were dull and half-closed.

The companions had followed Taran. As soon as Gurgi

saw what it was, he hunched up his shoulders, and with many fearful glances behind him, turned and crept off to a safe distance. Melyngar whinnied nervously. The white pig, undisturbed, sat on her haunches and looked cheerful.

Fflewddur, on seeing the bird, gave a low whistle. "It's a stroke of luck the parents aren't about," he said. "Those creatures will tear a man to shreds if their young are in danger."

"It reminds me of Achren," Eilonwy said, "especially around the eyes, on days when she was in a bad temper."

Doli pulled his axe from his belt.

"What are you going to do?" Taran asked.

The dwarf looked at him with surprise. "Going to do? Do you have any other stupid questions? You can't imagine I'd let it sit there, can you? I'm going to chop off its head, to begin with."

"No!" cried Taran, seizing the dwarf's arm. "It's badly hurt."

"Be glad of that," snapped Doli. "If it weren't, neither you nor I nor any of us would be standing here."

"I will not have it killed," Taran declared. "It's in pain and it needs help."

"That's true," Eilonwy said, "it doesn't look comfortable at all. For the matter of that, it looks even worse than Achren."

The dwarf threw his axe to the ground and put his

hands on his hips. "I can't make myself invisible," he snorted, "but at least I'm no fool. Go ahead. Pick up the vicious little thing. Give it a drink. Pat its head. Then you'll see what happens. As soon as it's got strength enough, the first thing it'll do is slice you to bits. And next thing, fly straight to Arawn. Then we'll be in a fine stew."

"What Doli says is true," Fflewddur added. "I myself don't enjoy chopping things up — the bird is interesting, in a disagreeable sort of way. But we've been lucky so far, with no trouble from gwythaints, at least. I don't see the use of bringing one of Arawn's spies right into our bosom, as you might say. A Fflam is always kind-hearted, but it seems to me this is overdoing it."

"Medwyn would not say so," Taran answered. "In the hills, he spoke of kindness for all creatures; and he told me much about the gwythaints. I think it's important to bring this one to Caer Dathyl. No one has ever captured a live gwythaint, as far as I know. Who can tell what value it may have?"

The bard scratched his head. "Well, yes, I suppose if it had any use at all, it would be better alive than dead. But the proposition is risky, no matter what."

Taran gestured for the others to stand away from the bush. He saw the gwythaint was wounded by more than thorns; perhaps an eagle had challenged it, for blood flecked its back and a number of feathers had been torn out.

He reached in carefully. The gwythaint hissed again, and a long, rasping rattle sounded in its throat. Taran feared the bird might be dying even then. He put a hand under its feverish body. The gwythaint struck with beak and talons, but its strength had gone. Taran lifted it free of the thornbush.

"If I can find the right herbs, I'll make a poultice," Taran told Eilonwy. "But I'll need hot water to steep them." While the girl prepared a nest of grass and leaves, Taran asked Gurgi to build a fire and heat some stones, which could be dropped into a cup of water. Then, with Hen Wen at his heels, he quickly set out to search for the plants.

"How long are we going to stay here?" Doli shouted after him. "Not that I care. You're the ones in a hurry, not I. Humph!" He thrust his axe into his belt, jammed his cap tight on his head, and furiously held his breath.

Taran was again grateful for what Coll had taught him of herbs. He found most of what he needed growing nearby. Hen Wen joined the hunt with enthusiasm, grunting happily, rooting under leaves and stones. Indeed, the white pig was the first to discover an important variety Taran had overlooked.

The gwythaint did not struggle when Taran applied the poultice; soaking a piece of cloth torn from his jacket in another healing brew, he squeezed the liquid drop by drop into the bird's beak.

"That's all very well," said Doli, whose curiosity had got the better of him, and who had come to observe the operation. "How do you imagine you'll carry the nasty thing — perched on your shoulder?"

"I don't know," Taran said. "I thought I could wrap it in my cloak."

Doli snorted. "That's the trouble with you great clodhoppers. You don't see beyond your noses. But if you expect me to build a cage for you, you're mistaken."

"A cage would be just the thing," Taran agreed. "No, I wouldn't want to bother you with that. I'll try to make one myself."

The dwarf watched contemptuously while Taran gathered saplings and attempted to weave them together.

"Oh, stop it!" Doli finally burst out. "I can't stand looking at botched work. Here, get out of the way." He shouldered Taran aside, squatted on the ground, and picked up the saplings. He trimmed them expertly with his knife, lashed them with braided vines, and in no time at all the dwarf held up a serviceable cage.

"That's certainly more practical than making yourself invisible," Eilonwy said.

The dwarf made no answer and only looked at her angrily.

Taran lined the bottom of the cage with leaves, gently put the gwythaint inside, and they resumed their march.

Doli now led them at a faster pace, to make up for the time they had lost. He tramped steadily down the hill slopes without even turning to see whether Taran and the others were able to keep up with him. The speed of their pace, Taran realized, served little purpose, since they were obliged to halt more frequently. But he did not deem it wise to mention this to the dwarf.

Throughout the day the gwythaint steadily improved. At each halt, Taran fed the bird and applied the medicines. Gurgi was still too terrified to come near; Taran alone dared handle the creature. When Fflewddur, endeavouring to make friends, put his finger into the cage, the gwythaint roused and slashed at him with its beak.

"I warn you," snapped Doli, "no good will come of this. But don't pay any attention to what I say. Go right ahead. Cut your own throats. Then come running and complaining afterwards. I'm just a guide; I do what I'm ordered to, and that's all."

At nightfall they made camp and discussed plans for the morrow. The gwythaint had entirely recovered, and had also developed an enormous appetite. It squawked furiously when Taran did not bring its food quickly enough, and rattled its beak against the cage. It gobbled up the morsels Taran gave it, then looked around for more. After eating, the gwythaint crouched at the bottom of the cage, its head cocked and listening, its eyes following every movement.

Taran finally ventured to put a finger past the bars and scratch the gwythaint's head. The creature no longer hissed, and it made no attempt to bite him. The gwythaint even allowed Eilonwy to feed it, but the bard's attempts to make friends failed.

"It knows perfectly well you'd agreed to chop off its head," Eilonwy told Fflewddur, "so you can't blame the poor thing for being annoyed at you. If somebody wanted to chop off *my* head, then came around afterwards and wanted to be sociable, I'd peck at him too."

"Gwydion told me the birds are trained when young," Taran said. "I wish he were here. He would know best how to handle the creature. Perhaps it could be taught differently. But there's bound to be a good falconer at Caer Dathyl, and we'll see what he can do."

But next morning, the cage was empty.

Doli, who had risen long before the others, was the first to discover it. The furious dwarf thrust the cage under Taran's nose. The sapling bars had been slashed to pieces by the gwythaint's beak.

"And there you have it!" cried Doli. "I told you so! Don't say I didn't warn you. The treacherous creature's halfway to Annuvin by now, after listening to every word we said. If Arawn didn't know where we are, he'll know soon enough. You've done well; oh, very well," Doli snorted. "Spare me from fools and Assistant Pig-Keepers!"

Taran could not hide his disappointment or fear.

Fflewddur said nothing, but the bard's face was grim.

"I've done the wrong thing again, as usual," Taran said angrily. "Doli is right. There's no difference between a fool and an Assistant Pig-Keeper."

"That's probably true," agreed Eilonwy, whose remark did nothing to cheer Taran. "But," she went on, "I can't stand people who say 'I told you so'. That's worse than somebody coming up and eating your dinner before you have a chance to sit down.

"Even so," she added, "Doli means well. He's not half as disagreeable as he pretends to be, and I'm sure he's worried about us. He's like a porcupine, all prickly on the outside, but very ticklish once you turn him over. If he'd only stop trying to make himself invisible, I think it should do a lot to improve his disposition."

There was no time for further regrets. Doli set them an even swifter pace. They still followed the hills along the Ystrad valley, but at midday the dwarf turned west and once more began to descend towards the plains. The sky had grown as thick and grey as lead. Violent gusts of wind whipped their faces. The pale sun gave no warmth. Melyngar neighed uneasily; Hen Wen, placid and agreeable until now, began to roll her eyes and mutter to herself.

While the companions rested briefly, Doli went ahead to scout the land. In a short time he was back again. He led them to the crest of a hill, motioned them to stay close to the ground, and pointed towards the Ystrad below.

The plain was covered with warriors, on foot and on horseback. Black banners snapped in the wind. Even at this distance, Taran could hear the clank of weapons, the steady, heavy drumming of marching feet. At the head of the winding columns rode the Horned King.

The giant figure towered above the men-at-arms, who galloped behind him. The curving antlers rose like eager claws. As Taran watched, terrified but unable to turn away, the Horned King's head swung slowly in the direction of the heights. Taran pressed flat against the earth. Arawn's champion, he was sure, could not see him; it was only a trick of his mind, a mirror of his own fear, but it seemed the Horned King's eyes sought him out and thrust like daggers at his heart.

"They have overtaken us," Taran said in a flat voice.

"Hurry," snapped the dwarf. "Get hustling, instead of dawdling and moaning. We're no more than a day away from Caer Dathyl and so are they. We can still move faster. If you hadn't stopped for the ungrateful spy of Annuvin, we'd be well ahead of them by now. Don't say I didn't warn you."

"We should arm ourselves a little better," the bard said. "The Horned King will have outriders on both sides of the valley."

Taran unstrapped the weapons on Melyngar's back and handed a bow and quiver of arrows to his companions, as well as a short spear for each. King Eiddileg had given them round bronze bucklers; they were dwarf-size and, after his view of the marching hosts, Taran found them pitifully small. Gurgi buckled a short sword around his waist. Of all the band, he was the most excited.

"Yes, yes!" he cried. "Now bold, valiant Gurgi is a mighty warrior, too! He has a grinding gasher and a pointed piercer! He is ready for great fightings and smitings!"

"And so am I!" Fflewddur declared. "Nothing withstands the onslaught of an angry Fflam!"

The dwarf clapped his hands to his head and gnashed his teeth. "Stop jabbering and move!" he sputtered. This time he was too furious to hold his breath.

Taran slung the buckler over his shoulder. Hen Wen hung back and grunted fearfully. "I know you're afraid," Taran whispered coaxingly, "but you'll be safe in Caer Dathyl."

The pig followed reluctantly; but as Doli set off once again, she lagged behind, and it was all Taran could do to urge her forwards. Her pink snout trembled; her eyes darted from one side of the path to the other.

At the next halt Doli summoned Taran. "Keep on like this," he cried, "and you'll have no chance at all. First a gwythaint delays us, now a pig!"

"She's frightened," Taran tried to explain to the angry dwarf. "She knows the Horned King is near."

"Then tie her up," Doli said. "Put her on the horse."

Taran nodded. "Yes. She won't like it, but there's nothing else we can do."

A few moments before, the pig had been crouched at the roots of a tree. Now there was no sign of her.

"Hen?" Taran called. He turned to the bard. "Where did she go?" he asked in alarm.

The bard shook his head. Neither he nor Eilonwy had seen her move; Gurgi had been watering Melyngar and had not noticed the pig at all.

"She can't have run off again," Taran cried. He raced back into the woods. When he returned, his face was pale.

"She's gone," he gasped. "She's hiding somewhere, I know it."

He sank to the ground and put his head in his hands. "I shouldn't have let her out of my sight, not even for a moment," he said bitterly. "I have failed twice."

"Let the others go on," Eilonwy said. "We'll find her and catch up with them."

Before Taran could answer, he heard a sound that chilled his blood. From the hills came the voices of a hunting pack in full cry and the long notes of a horn.

The companions stood frozen with dread. With the ice of terror in his throat, Taran looked at the silent faces around him. The dire music trembled in the air; a shadow flickered across the lowering sky.

"Where Gwyn the Hunter rides," murmured Fflewddur, "death rides close behind."

CHAPTER EIGHTEEN

The Flame of Dyrnwyn

No sooner had the notes of Gwyn's horn sunk into the hills than Taran started, as though waking from a fearful dream. Hoofbeats drummed across the meadow.

"The Horned King's scouts!" cried Fflewddur, pointing to the mounted warriors galloping towards them. "They've seen us!"

Up from the plains the riders sped, bent over their saddles, urging on their steeds. They drew closer, lances levelled as if each gleaming point sought its own target.

"I could try to make another web," Eilonwy suggested, then added, "but I'm afraid the last one wasn't too useful."

Taran's sword flashed out. "There are only four of them," he said. "We match them in numbers at least."

"Put up your blade," Fflewddur said. "Arrows first. We'll have work enough for swords later."

They unslung their bows. Under Fflewddur's orders, they formed a line and kneeled shoulder to shoulder. The bard's spiky yellow hair blew in the wind; his face shone with excitement. "I haven't had a good fight in years," he said. "That's one of the things I miss, being a bard. They'll see what it means to attack a Fflam!"

Taran nocked an arrow to the string. At a word from the bard, the companions drew their bows and took aim.

"Loose!" shouted Fflewddur.

Taran saw his own shaft fly wide of the leading horseman. With a cry of anger, he seized another arrow from the quiver. Beside him, he heard Gurgi shout triumphantly. Of the volley, only Gurgi's bolt had found its mark. A warrior toppled from his horse, the shaft deep in his throat.

"They know we can sting!" Fflewddur cried. "Loose again!"

The horsemen veered. More cautious now, the warriors raised their bucklers. Of the three, two drove directly for the companions; the third turned his mount's head and galloped to the flank of the defenders.

"Now, friends," shouted the bard, "back to back!"

Taran heard Doli grunt as the dwarf loosed an arrow at the nearest warrior. Gurgi's shot had been lucky; now the shafts hissed through the air only to glance off the attackers' light shields. Behind Taran, Melyngar whinnied and pawed the ground frantically. Taran remembered how valiantly she had fought for Gwydion, but she was tethered now and he dared not break away from the defenders to untie her.

The horsemen circled. One turned his exposed side to the companions. Doli's arrow leaped from the bowstring and buried itself in the warrior's neck. The other horsemen spun their mounts and galloped across the meadow.

"We've beaten them!" cried Eilonwy. "That's like bees driving away eagles!"

The panting Fflewddur shook his head. "They'll spend no more men on us. When they come back, they'll come back with a war band. That's highly complimentary to our bravery, but I don't think we should wait for them. A Fflam knows when to fight and when to run. At this point, we had better run."

"I won't leave Hen Wen," cried Taran.

"Go look for her," growled Doli. "You'll lose your head as well as your pig."

"Crafty Gurgi will go," suggested Gurgi, "with bold seekings and peekings."

"In all likelihood," said the bard, "they'll attack us again. We can't afford to lose what little strength we have. A Fflam never worries about being outnumbered, but one sword less could be fatal. I'm sure your pig is able to look out for herself; wherever she may be, she is in less danger than we are."

Taran nodded. "It is true. But it grieves me to lose her for the second time. I had chosen to abandon my search and go to Caer Dathyl; then, after Gurgi found Hen Wen, I had hoped to accomplish both tasks. But I fear it must be one or the other."

"The question is," said Fflewddur, "is there any chance at all of warning the Sons of Don before the Horned King attacks? Doli is the only one who can answer that."

The dwarf scowled and thought for a few moments. "Possible," he said, "but we'll have to go into the valley. We'll be in the middle of the Horned King's vanguard if we do."

"Can we get through?" asked Taran.

"Won't know until you've tried," grunted Doli.

"The decision is yours," said the bard, glancing at Taran.

"We shall try," Taran answered.

For the rest of that day they travelled without a halt. At nightfall, Taran would have been glad to rest, but the dwarf warned against it. The companions pressed on in weary silence. They had escaped the attack Fflewddur expected, but a column of horsemen bearing torches passed within bowshot of them. The companions crouched in the fringe of trees until the streaks of flame wound behind a hill and vanished. In a short time, Doli led the little band into the valley, where they found concealment in the wooded groves.

But the dawn revealed a sight that filled Taran with despair. The valley roiled with warriors wherever he turned his eyes. Black banners whipped against the sky. The host of the Horned King was like the body of an armed giant restlessly stirring.

For a moment, Taran stared in disbelief. He turned his face away. "Too late," he murmured. "Too late. We have failed."

While the dwarf surveyed the marching columns, Fflewddur strode forwards. "There is one thing we can do," he cried. "Caer Dathyl lies straight ahead. Let us go on, and make our last stand there."

Taran nodded. "Yes. My place is at the side of Gwydion's people. Doli shall lead Gurgi and Eilonwy to safety." He took a deep breath and buckled his sword belt more tightly. "You have guided us well," he said quietly to the dwarf.

"Return to your king with our gratitude. Your work is done."

The dwarf looked at him furiously. "Done!" he snorted. "Idiots and numbskulls! It's not that I care what happens to you, but don't think I'm going to watch you get hacked to pieces. I can't stand a botched job. Like it or not, I'm going with you."

Before the words were out of his mouth, an arrow sang past Doli's head. Melyngar reared up. A party of foot soldiers sprang from the woods behind the companions. "Begone!" the bard shouted to Taran. "Ride as fast as you can, or it will be death for all of us!"

When Taran hesitated, the bard seized him by the shoulders, pitched him towards the horse, and thrust Eilonwy after him. Fflewddur drew his sword. "Do as I say!" shouted the bard, his eyes blazing.

Taran leaped to Melyngar's saddle and pulled Eilonwy up behind him. The white horse shot forwards. Eilonwy clung to Taran's waist as the steed galloped straight across the bracken, towards the vanguard of the Horned King. Taran made no attempt to guide her; the horse had chosen her own path. Suddenly he was in the midst of the warriors. Melyngar reared and plunged. Taran's sword was out and he struck right and left. A hand clutched at the stirrups, then was ripped away. Taran saw the warrior stumble back and drown in the press of struggling men. The white horse broke free and streaked for the brow of the hill. One mounted figure galloped behind them now. In a terrified glance, Taran saw the sweeping antlers of the Horned King.

The black steed gained on them. Melyngar turned sharply and drove towards the forest. The Horned King turned with her, and as they crashed through the underbrush and past the first rows of trees, the antlered giant drew closer until both steeds galloped side by side. In a final burst of speed, the horse of the Horned King plunged ahead; the animal's flanks bore against Melyngar, who reared furiously and struck out with her hoofs. Taran and Eilonwy were flung from the saddle. The Horned King turned his mount, seeking to trample them.

Taran scrambled to his feet and struck blindly with his sword. Then, gripping Eilonwy's arm, he pulled her deeper into the protection of the trees. The Horned King sprang heavily to the ground and was upon them in a few long strides.

Eilonwy screamed. Taran swung about to face the antlered man. Dark fears clutched Taran, as though the Lord of Annuvin himself had opened an abyss at his feet and he was hurtling downwards. He gasped with pain, as though his old wound had opened up once again. All the despair he had known as Achren's captive returned to sap his strength.

Behind the bleached skull, the eyes of the Horned King flamed, as he raised a crimson-stained arm.

Blindly, Taran brought up his sword. It trembled in his hand. The Horned King's blade lashed against the weapon and shattered it with a single blow.

Taran dropped the useless shards. The Horned King paused, a growl of savage joy rose in his throat, and he took a firmer grasp on his weapon.

Mortal terror goaded Taran into action. He leaped back and spun towards Eilonwy. "Dyrnwyn!" he cried. "Give me the sword!"

Before she could move, he tore the belt and weapon from her shoulder. The Horned King saw the black scabbard and hesitated a moment, as if in fear.

Taran grasped the hilt. The blade would not come free. He pulled with all his strength. The sword moved only a little from its sheath. The Horned King raised his own weapon. As Taran gave a final wrench, the scabbard turned in his hand. A blinding flash split the air in front of him. Lightning seared his arm and he was thrown violently to the ground.

The sword Dyrnwyn, blazing white with flame, leaped from his hand, and fell beyond his reach. The Horned King stood over him. With a cry, Eilonwy sprang at the antlered man. Snarling, the giant tossed her aside.

A voice rang out behind the Horned King. Through

eyes blurred with pain, Taran glimpsed a tall figure against the trees, and heard a shouted word he could not distinguish.

The Horned King stood motionless, his arm upraised. Lightning played about his sword. The giant flamed like a burning tree. The stag horns turned to crimson streaks, the skull mask ran like molten iron. A roar of pain and rage rose from the Antlered King's throat.

With a cry, Taran flung an arm across his face. The ground rumbled and seemed to open beneath him. Then there was nothing.

CHAPTER NINETEEN

The Secret

Sunlight streamed through the high window of a chamber pleasantly cool and fragrant. Taran blinked and tried to lift himself from the low, narrow couch. His head spun; his arm, swathed in white linen, throbbed painfully. Dry rushes covered the floor; the bright rays turned them yellow as wheat. Beside the couch, a white, sun-dappled shape stirred and rose up.

"Hwoinch!"

Hen Wen, wheezing and chuckling, grinned all over her

round face. With a joyful grunt, she began nuzzling Taran's cheek. His mouth opened, but he could not speak. A silvery laugh rang from a corner of the chamber.

"You should really see your expression. You look like a fish that's climbed into a bird's nest by mistake."

Eilonwy rose from the osier stool. "I was hoping you'd wake up soon. You can't imagine how boring it is to sit and watch somebody sleep. It's like counting stones in a wall."

"Where have they taken us? Is this Annuvin?"

Eilonwy laughed again and shook her head. "That's exactly the sort of question you might expect from an Assistant Pig-Keeper. Annuvin? Ugh! I wouldn't want to be there at all. Why must you always think of unpleasant things? I suppose it's because your wound probably did something to your head. You're looking a lot better now than you did, though you still have that greenish-white colour, like a boiled leek."

"Stop chattering and tell me where we are!" Taran tried to roll from the couch, then sank back weakly and put a hand to his head.

"You aren't supposed to get up yet," Eilonwy cautioned, "but I imagine you've just discovered that for yourself."

Wriggling and grunting loudly, the delighted Hen Wen had begun to climb onto the couch. Eilonwy snapped her fingers. "Stop that, Hen," she ordered, "you know he isn't to be disturbed or upset and especially not sat on." The girl turned again to Taran. "We're in Caer Dathyl," she said. "It's a lovely place. Much nicer than Spiral Castle."

Taran started up once more as memories flooded over him. "The Horned King!" he cried. "What happened? Where is he?"

"In a barrow, most likely, I should think."

"Is he dead?"

"Naturally," answered the girl. "You don't think he'd stand being put in a barrow if he weren't, do you? There wasn't a great deal left of him, but what there was got buried." Eilonwy shuddered. "I think he was the most terrifying person I've ever met, and that includes Achren. He gave me a dreadful tossing about – just before he was going to smite you." She rubbed her head. "For the matter of that, you pulled away my sword rather roughly. I told you and told you not to draw it. But you wouldn't listen. That's what burned your arm."

Taran noticed the black scabbard of Dyrnwyn no longer hung from Eilonwy's shoulder. "But then what..."

"It's lucky you went unconscious," Eilonwy continued. "You missed the worst of it. There was the earthquake, and the Horned King burning until he just, well, broke apart. It wasn't pleasant. The truth of the matter is, I'd rather not talk about it. It still gives me bad dreams, even when I'm not asleep."

Taran gritted his teeth. "Eilonwy," he said at last, "I

want you to tell me very slowly and carefully what happened. If you don't, *I'm* going to be angry and *you're* going to be sorry."

"How – can – I – tell – you – anything," Eilonwy said, deliberately pronouncing every word and making extravagant grimaces as she did so, "if – you – don't – want – me – to – talk?" She shrugged. "Well, in any case," she resumed, at her usual breathless rate, "as soon as the armies saw the Horned King was dead, they practically fell apart, too. Not the same way, naturally. With them, it was more sort of running away, like a herd of rabbits – no, that isn't right, is it? But it was pitiful to see grown men so frightened. Of course, by that time the Sons of Don had their chance to attack. You should have seen the golden banners. And such handsome warriors." Eilonwy sighed. "It was – it was like – I don't even know what it was like."

"And Hen Wen..."

"She hasn't stirred from this chamber ever since they brought you here," said Eilonwy. "Neither have I," she added, with a glance at Taran. "She's a very intelligent pig," Eilonwy went on. "Oh, she does get frightened and loses her head once in a while, I suppose. And she can be very stubborn when she wants, which sometimes makes me wonder how much difference there is between pigs and people who keep them. I'm not mentioning anyone in particular, you understand."

The door opposite Taran's couch opened part way. Around it appeared the spiky yellow head and pointed nose of Fflewddur Fflam.

"So you're back with us," cried the bard. "Or, as you might say, we're back with you!"

Gurgi and the dwarf, who had been standing behind the bard, now rushed in; despite Eilonwy's protests, they crowded around Taran. Fflewddur and Doli showed no sign of injury, but Gurgi's head was bound up and he moved with a limp.

"Yes! Yes!" he cried. "Gurgi fought for his friend with slashings and gashings! What smitings! Fierce warriors strike him about his poor tender head, but valiant Gurgi does not flee, oh, no!"

Taran smiled at him, deeply touched. "I'm sorry about your poor tender head," he said, putting a hand on Gurgi's shoulder, "and that a friend should be wounded for my sake."

"What joy! What clashings and smashings! Ferocious Gurgi fills wicked warriors with awful terror and outcries."

"It's true," said the bard. "He was the bravest of us all. Though my stumpy friend here can do surprising things with an axe."

Doli, for the first time, grinned. "Never thought any of you had any mettle to show," he said, attempting to be gruff. "Took you all for milksops at first. Deepest apologies," he added, with a bow.

"We held off the war band," Fflewddur said, "until we were sure you were well away. Some of them should have occasion to think unkindly of us for a while to come." The bard's face lit up. "There we were," he cried, "fighting like madmen, hopelessly outnumbered. But a Fflam never surrenders! I took on three at once. Slash! Thrust! Another seized me from behind, the wretched coward. But I flung him off. We disengaged them and made for Caer Dathyl, chopping and hacking all the way, beset on all sides..."

Taran expected Fflewddur's harp strings to sunder at any moment. To his surprise, they held firm.

"And so," Fflewddur concluded with a carefree shrug, "that was our part. Rather easy, when you come down to it; I had no fear of things going badly, not for an instant."

A string broke with a deep twang.

Fflewddur bent down to Taran. "Terrified," he whispered. "Absolutely green."

Eilonwy seized the bard and thrust him towards the door. "Begone!" she cried. "All of you! You'll wear him out with your chatter." The girl shoved Gurgi and the dwarf after Fflewddur. "And stay out! No one's to come in until I say they can."

"Not even I?"

Taran started up at the familiar voice.

Gwydion stood in the doorway.

For a moment Taran did not recognize him. Instead of

the stained cloak and coarse jacket, Gwydion wore the shining raiment of a prince. His rich mantle hung in deep folds. On a chain at his throat gleamed a sun-shaped disc of gold. His green eyes shone with new depth and power. Taran saw him now as he had always imagined him.

Heedless of his wounded arm, Taran sprang from the couch. The tall figure strode towards him. The authority of the warrior's bearing made Taran drop to one knee. "Lord Gwydion," he murmured.

"That is no greeting from a friend to a friend," said Gwydion, gently raising Taran to his feet. "It gives me more pleasure to remember an Assistant Pig-Keeper who feared I would poison him in the forest near Caer Dallben."

"After Spiral Castle," Taran stammered, "I never thought to see you alive." He clasped Gwydion's hand and wept unashamedly.

"A little more alive than you are." Gwydion smiled. He helped Taran seat himself on the couch.

"But how did..." Taran began, as he noticed a black and battered weapon at Gwydion's side.

Gwydion saw the question on Taran's face. "A gift," he said, "a royal gift from a young lady."

"I girded it on him myself," Eilonwy interrupted. She turned to Gwydion. "I told him not to draw it, but he's impossibly stubborn."

"Fortunately you did not unsheathe it entirely," Gwydion

said to Taran. "I fear the flame of Dyrnwyn would have been too great even for an Assistant Pig-Keeper.

"It is a weapon of power, as Eilonwy recognized," Gwydion added. "So ancient that I believed it no more than a legend. There are still deep secrets concerning Dyrnwyn, unknown even to the wisest. Its loss destroyed Spiral Castle and was a severe blow to Arawn."

With a single, firm gesture, Gwydion drew the blade and held it aloft. The weapon glittered blindingly. In fear and wonder, Taran shrank back, his wound throbbing anew. Gwydion quickly returned the blade to its scabbard.

"As soon as I saw Lord Gwydion," Eilonwy put in, with an admiring glance at him, "I knew he was the one who should keep the sword. I must say I'm glad to have done with the clumsy thing."

"Do stop interrupting," Taran cried. "Let me find out what happened to my friend before you start babbling."

"I shall not weary you with a long tale," Gwydion said. "You already know Arawn's threat has been turned aside. He may strike again, how or when no man can guess. But for the moment there is little fear."

"What of Achren?" Taran asked. "And Spiral Castle..."

"I was not in Spiral Castle when it crumbled," Gwydion said. "Achren took me from my cell and bound me to a horse. With the Cauldron-Born, we rode to the castle of Oeth-Anoeth."

"Oeth-Anoeth?" questioned Taran.

"Yet, before she thrust me into its dungeons, she gripped my arm. 'Why do you choose death, Lord Gwydion,' she cried, 'when I can offer you eternal life and power beyond the grasp of mortal minds?'

"'I ruled Prydain long before Arawn,' Achren told me, 'and it was I who made him king over Annuvin. It was I who gave him power – though he used it to betray me. But now, if you desire it, you shall take your place on the high throne of Arawn himself and rule in his stead.'

"'Gladly will I overthrow Arawn,' I answered. 'And I will use those powers to destroy you along with him.'

"Raging, she cast me into the lowest dungeon," Gwydion said. "I have never been closer to death than in Oeth-Anoeth.

"How long I lay there, I cannot be sure," Gwydion continued. "In Oeth-Anoeth, time is not as you know it here. It is better that I do not speak of the torments Achren had devised. The worst were not of the body but of the spirit, and of these the most painful was despair. Yet, even in my deepest anguish, I clung to hope. For there is this about Oeth-Anoeth: if a man withstand it, even death will give up its secrets to him.

"I withstood it," Gwydion said quietly, "and at the end much was revealed to me which before had been clouded. Of this, too, I shall not speak. It is enough for you to know that I understood the workings of life and death, of laughter and tears, endings and beginnings. I saw the truth of the world, and knew no chains could hold me. My bonds were light as dreams. At that moment, the walls of my prison melted."

"What became of Achren?" Eilonwy asked.

"I do not know," Gwydion said. "I did not see her thereafter. For some days I lay concealed in the forest, to heal the injuries of my body. Spiral Castle was in ruins when I returned to seek you; and there I mourned your death."

"As we mourned yours," Taran said.

"I set out for Caer Dathyl again," Gwydion continued. "For a time I followed the same path Fflewddur chose for you, though I did not cross the valley until much later. By then, I had outdistanced you a little.

"That day, a gwythaint plunged from the sky and flew directly towards me. To my surprise, it neither attacked nor sped away after it had seen me, but fluttered before me, crying strangely. The gwythaint's language is no longer secret to me — nor is the speech of any living creature — and I understood a band of travellers was journeying from the hills nearby and a white pig accompanied them.

"I hastened to retrace my steps. By then, Hen Wen sensed I was close at hand. When she ran from you," Gwydion said to Taran, "she ran not in terror but to find me. What I learned from her was more important than I suspected, and I understood why Arawn's champion sought her desperately. He, too, realized she knew the one thing that could destroy him."

"What was that?" Taran asked urgently.

"She knew the Horned King's secret name."

"His name?" Taran cried in astonishment. "I never realized a name could be so powerful."

"Yes," Gwydion answered. "Once you have courage to look upon evil, seeing it for what it is and naming it by its true name, it is powerless against you, and you can destroy it. Yet, with all my understanding," he said, reaching down and scratching the white pig's ear, "I could not have discovered the Horned King's name without Hen Wen.

"Hen Wen told me this secret in the forest. I had no need of letter sticks or tomes of enchantment, for we could speak as one heart and mind to each other. The gwythaint, circling overhead, led me to the Horned King. The rest you know."

"Where is the gwythaint now?" asked Taran.

Gwydion shook his head. "I do not know. But I doubt she will ever return to Annuvin, for Arawn would rend her to pieces once he learned what she had done. I only know she has repaid your kindness in the fullest measure.

"Rest now," Gwydion said. "Later, we shall speak of happier things."

"Lord Gwydion," Eilonwy called, as he rose to leave, "what was the Horned King's secret name?"

Gwydion's lined face broke into a smile. "It must remain a secret," he said, then patted the girl gently on the cheek. "But I assure you, it was not half as pretty as your own."

A few days afterwards, when Taran had regained strength enough to walk unaided, Gwydion accompanied him through Caer Dathyl. Standing high on a hill, the fortress alone was big enough to hold several Caer Dallbens. Taran saw armourers' shops, stables for the steeds of warriors, breweries, weaving rooms. Cottages clustered in the valleys below, and clear streams ran golden in the sunlight. Later, Gwydion summoned all the companions to the Great Hall of Caer Dathyl, and there, amid banners and hedges of spears, they received the gratitude of King Math Son of Mathonwy, ruler of the House of Don. The white-bearded monarch, who looked as old as Dallben and as testy, was even more talkative than Eilonwy. But when at last he had finished one of the longest speeches Taran had ever heard, the companions bowed, and a guard of honour bore King Math from the Hall on a litter draped with cloth of gold. As Taran and his friends were about to take their leave, Gwydion called to them.

"These are small gifts for great valour," he said. "But it

is in my power to bestow them, which I do with a glad heart, and with hope that you will treasure them not so much for their value as for the sake of remembrance.

"To Fflewddur Fflam shall be given one harp string. Though all his others break, this shall for ever hold, regardless of how many gallant extravagances he may put on it. And its tone shall be the truest and most beautiful.

"To Doli of the Fair Folk shall be granted the power of invisibility, so long as he chooses to retain it.

"To faithful and valiant Gurgi shall be given a wallet of food which shall always be full. Guard it well; it is one of the treasures of Prydain.

"To Eilonwy of the House of Llyr shall be given a ring of gold set with a gem carved by the ancient craftsmen of the Fair Folk. It is precious; but to me, her friendship is even more precious.

"And to Taran of Caer Dallben..." Here, Gwydion paused. "The choice of his reward has been the most difficult of all."

"I ask no reward," Taran said. "I want no friend to repay me for what I did willingly, out of friendship and for my own honour."

Gwydion smiled. "Taran of Caer Dallben," he said, "you are still as touchy and headstrong as ever. Believe that I know what you yearn for in your heart. The dreams of heroism, of worth, and of achievement are noble ones; but you, not I, must make them come true. Ask me whatever else, and I shall grant it."

Taran bowed his head. "In spite of all that has befallen me, I have come to love the valleys and mountains of your northern lands. But my thoughts have turned more and more to Caer Dallben. I long to be home."

Gwydion nodded. "So it shall be."

CHAPTER TWENTY

Welcomes

The journey to Caer Dallben was swift and unhindered, for the lords of the southern cantrevs, their power broken, had slunk back each to his own tribe throne. Taran and his companions, with Gwydion himself leading, rode south through the Valley of Ystrad. Eilonwy, who had heard so much of Taran's talk of Coll and Dallben, would not be denied a visit, and she, too, rode with them. Gwydion had given each of the companions a handsome steed; to Taran he had given the finest: the grey, silver-maned stallion,

Melynlas, of the lineage of Melyngar and as swift. Hen Wen rode triumphantly on a horse-litter, looking intensely pleased with herself.

Caer Dallben had never seen so joyous a welcome — though by this time Taran was not positive about what Dallben had or had not seen — with such feasting that even Gurgi had his fill for once. Coll embraced Taran, who was amazed that such a hero would deign to remember an Assistant Pig-Keeper, as well as Eilonwy, Hen Wen, and anyone else he could get his hands on; his face beamed like a winter fire and his bald crown glowed with delight.

Dallben interrupted his meditations to be present at the feast; though soon after the festivities, he withdrew to his chamber and was not seen for some time. Later, he and Gwydion spent several hours alone, for there were important matters Gwydion would reveal only to the old enchanter.

Gurgi, making himself completely at home, snored under a pile of hay in the barn. While Fflewddur and Doli went off exploring, Taran showed Eilonwy Hen Wen's enclosure, where the pig chuckled and grunted as happily as before.

"So this is where it all began," Eilonwy said. "I don't want to sound critical, but I don't think you should have had all that trouble keeping her in. Caer Dallben is as lovely as you said, and you should be glad to be home," she went on. "It's like suddenly remembering where you put something you've been looking for."

"Yes, I suppose it is," Taran said, leaning on the railing and examining it closely.

"What will you do now?" asked Eilonwy. "I expect you'll go back to Assistant Pig-Keeping."

Without looking up, Taran nodded. "Eilonwy," he said, with hesitation, "I was hoping – I mean, I was wondering..."

Before he could finish, Coll came hurrying up and whispered that Dallben would like to see him privately.

"Eilonwy—" Taran began again, then stopped abruptly and strode off to the cottage.

When he entered the chamber, Dallben was writing with a great quill in *The Book of Three*. As soon as he saw Taran, he shut the volume quickly and put it aside.

"Well, now," Dallben said, "I should like the two of us to speak quietly to each other. First, I am interested to learn what you think of being a hero. I daresay you feel rather proud of yourself. Although," he added, "I do not gain that impression from your face."

"I have no just cause for pride," Taran said, taking his usual place on the familiar bench. "It was Gwydion who destroyed the Horned King, and Hen Wen helped him do it. But Gurgi, not I, found her. Doli and Fflewddur fought gloriously while I was wounded by a sword I had no right to draw. And Eilonwy was the one who took the sword from the barrow in the first place. As for me, what I mostly did was make mistakes."

"My, my," said Dallben, "those are complaints enough to dampen the merriest feast. Though what you say may be true, you have cause for a certain pride nevertheless. It was you who held the companions together and led them. You did what you set out to do, and Hen Wen is safely back with us. If you made mistakes, you recognize them. As I told you, there are times when the seeking counts more than the finding.

"Does it truly matter," Dallben went on, "which of you did what, since all shared the same goal and the same danger? Nothing we do is ever done entirely alone. There is a part of us in everyone else — you, of all people, should know that. From what I hear, you have been as impetuous as your friend Fflewddur; I have been told, among other things, of a night when you dived head first into a thornbush. And you have certainly felt as sorry for yourself as Gurgi; and, like Doli, striven for the impossible."

"Yes," admitted Taran, "but that is not all that troubles me. I have dreamed often of Caer Dallben and I love it — and you and Coll — more than ever. I asked for nothing better than to be at home, and my heart rejoices. Yet it is a curious feeling. I have returned to the chamber I slept in and found it smaller than I remember. The fields are beautiful, yet not quite as I recalled them. And I am troubled, for I wonder now if I am to be a stranger in my own home."

Dallben shook his head. "No, that you shall never be. But it is not Caer Dallben which has grown smaller. You have grown bigger. That is the way of it."

"And there is Eilonwy," Taran said. "What will become of her? Is it – is it possible you would let her stay with us?"

Dallben pursed his lips and toyed with the pages of *The Book of Three*. "By all rights," he said, "the Princess Eilonwy should be returned to her kinsmen – yes, she is a princess. Did she not tell you? But there is no hurry about that. She might consent to stay. Perhaps if you spoke to her."

Taran sprang to his feet. "I shall!"

He hurried from the chamber and ran to Hen Wen's enclosure. Eilonwy was still there, watching the oracular pig with interest.

"You're to stay!" Taran cried. "I've asked Dallben!"

Eilonwy tossed her head. "I suppose," she said, "it never occurred to you to ask *me*."

"Yes – but I mean..." he stammered, "I didn't think..."

"You usually don't," Eilonwy sighed. "No matter. Coll is straightening up a place for me."

"Already?" cried Taran. "How did *he* know? How did *you* know?"

"Humph!" said Eilonwy.

"Hwoinch!" said Hen Wen.

Prydain Pronunciation Guide

Achren	~	*AHK-ren*
Adaon	~	*ah-DAY-on*
Aeddan	~	*EE-dan*
Angharad	~	*an-GAR-ad*
Annuvin	~	*ah-NOO-vin*
Arawn	~	*ah-RAWN*
Arianllyn	~	*ahree-AHN-lin*
Briavael	~	*bree-AH-vel*
Brynach	~	*BRIHN-ak*
Caer Cadarn	~	*kare KAH-darn*
Caer Colur	~	*kare KOH-loor*
Caer Dathyl	~	*kare DA-thil*
Coll	~	*kahl*
Dallben	~	*DAHL-ben*
Doli	~	*DOH-lee*
Don	~	*dahn*
Dwyvach	~	*DWIH-vak*
Dyrnwyn	~	*DUHRN-win*

Edyrnion	~	*eh-DIR-nyon*
Eiddileg	~	*eye-DILL-eg*
Eilonwy	~	*eye-LAHN-wee*
Ellidyr	~	*ELLI-deer*
Fflewddur Fflam	~	*FLEW-der flam*
Geraint	~	*GHER-aint*
Goewin	~	*GOH-win*
Govannion	~	*go-VAH-nyon*
Gurgi	~	*GHER-ghee*
Gwydion	~	*GWIH-dyon*
Gwythaint	~	*GWIH-thaint*
Islimach	~	*iss-LIM-ahk*
Llawgadarn	~	*law-GAD-arn*
Lluagor	~	*lew-AH-gore*
Llunet	~	*LOO-net*
Llyan	~	*lee-AHN*
Llyr	~	leer

Melyngar	~	*MELLIN-gar*
Melynlas	~	*MELLIN-lass*
Oeth-Anoeth	~	*eth-AHN-eth*
Orddu	~	*OR-doo*
Orgoch	~	*OR-gahk*
Orwen	~	*OR-wen*
Prydain	~	*prih-DANE*
Pryderi	~	*prih-DAY-ree*
Rhuddlum	~	*ROOD-lum*
Rhun	~	*roon*
Smoit	~	*smoyt*
Taliesin	~	*tally-ESS-in*
Taran	~	*TAH-ran*
Teleria	~	*tell-EHR-ya*

Author's Note

This chronicle of the Land of Prydain is not a retelling or
retranslation of Welsh mythology. Prydain is not Wales —
not entirely, at least. The inspiration for it comes from that
magnificent land and its legends; but, essentially, Prydain is
a country existing only in the imagination.

A few of its inhabitants are drawn from the ancient
tales. Gwydion, for example, is a "real" legendary figure.
Arawn, the dread Lord of Annuvin, comes from the
Mabinogion, the classic collection of Welsh legends, though
in Prydain he is considerably more villainous. And there is
an authentic mythological basis for Arawn's cauldron, Hen
Wen the oracular pig, the old enchanter Dallben, and
others. However, Taran the Assistant Pig-Keeper, like
Eilonwy of the red-gold hair, was born in my own Prydain.

The geography of Prydain is peculiar to itself. Any
resemblance between it and Wales is perhaps not coincidental
— but not to be used as a guide for tourists. It is a small
land, yet it has room enough for gallantry and humour; and
even an Assistant Pig-Keeper there may cherish certain
dreams.

The chronicle of Prydain is a fantasy. Such things never happen in real life. Or do they? Most of us are called on to perform tasks far beyond what we can do. Our capabilities seldom match our aspirations, and we are often woefully unprepared. To this extent, we are all Assistant Pig-Keepers at heart.

Lloyd Alexander

LLOYD ALEXANDER is one of the most respected and best-loved of American authors, with a huge following worldwide. *The Chronicles of Prydain* have won many awards, including the highly prestigious Newbery Medal for *The High King*, as well as the Newbery Honour for *The Black Cauldron* and the ALA Notable Book for *The Book of Three*. He is best known for his tales of high fantasy and adventure, and in 2003 he was awarded a Life Achievement Award by the World Fantasy Convention.

Born 30th January 1924 – Died 17th May 2007

"I never became a world traveller, an explorer, an adventurer. But I did become a writer, which is pretty much the same thing."

Lloyd Alexander

USBORNE MODERN CLASSICS

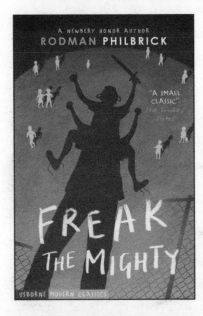

UNLIKELY PAIR
UNFORGETTABLE
FRIENDSHIP

AWARD-WINNER
TEAR-JERKER

HISTORICAL FICTION
RELEVANT NOW

Introducing timeless stories to today's readers

PAGE-TURNER
PRIZE-WINNER

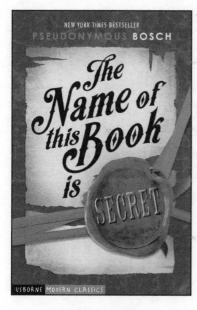

RIB-TICKLER
BEST-SELLER

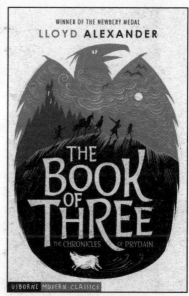

CULT CLASSIC
TIMELESS ADVENTURE